Kiss Me like you Mean It, COWBOY

CAVANAGH COWBOYS ROMANCE - 4

VALERIE COMER

Greenwords Media

Valerie Comer Bibliography

Urban Farm Fresh Romance

0. Promise of Peppermint (ebook only)
1. Secrets of Sunbeams
2. Butterflies on Breezes
3. Memories of Mist
4. Wishes on Wildflowers
5. Flavors of Forever
6. Raindrops on Radishes
7. Dancing at Daybreak
8. Glimpses of Gossamer
9. Lavished with Lavender
10. Cadence of Cranberries
11. Joys of Juniper
12. Together in Thyme

Pot of Gold Geocaching Romance

1. Topaz Treasure
2. Ruby Radiance
3. Sapphire Sentiments
4. Amethyst Attraction

Miss Snowflake Pageant

1. More Than a Tiara
2. Other Than a Halo
3. Better Than a Crown

Farm Fresh Romance

1. Raspberries and Vinegar
2. Wild Mint Tea
3. Sweetened with Honey
4. Dandelions for Dinner
5. Plum Upside Down
6. Berry on Top

Cavanagh Cowboys Romance
(Montana Ranches Christian Romance)

1. Marry Me for Real, Cowboy'
2. Give Me Another Chance, Cowboy
3. Let Me Off Easy, Cowboy
4. Kiss Me Like You Mean It, Cowboy

Saddle Springs Romance
(Montana Ranches Christian Romance)

1. The Cowboy's Christmas Reunion
2. The Cowboy's Mixed-Up Matchmaker
3. The Cowboy's Romantic Dreamer
4. The Cowboy's Convenient Marriage
5. The Cowboy's Belated Discovery
6. The Cowboy's Reluctant Bride

Garden Grown Romance
(Arcadia Valley Romance)

1. Sown in Love (ebook only)
2. Sprouts of Love
3. Rooted in Love
4. Harvest of Love

Riverbend Romance Novellas

1. Secretly Yours
2. Pinky Promise
3. Sweet Serenade
4. Team Bride
5. Merry Kisses

valeriecomer.com/books

CHAPTER ONE

That's enough. I'm done."

Yikes. Blake Cavanagh winced back a step as Felicity McKnight pressed forward. Her eyes blazed, and her normally pale cheeks had mottled in anger. Her finger jabbed repeatedly into his chest like a woodpecker determined to get to the heart of a big old cedar in two minutes flat.

"Okay, okay. I'm sorry." He held up both hands.

"You don't get it, do you?" She grabbed a handful of his snap-front shirt.

Not really, but he knew better than to say the words. "You're done. That's clear enough. I thought we had an arrangement..." Oops. Wrong answer.

Her lips drew into a tight line that was not at all kissable. "Casual dating. No commitment. That was fine. I didn't want to marry you, anyway."

That made two of them. Not only did Blake not wish to marry Felicity, he wasn't planning on marrying anyone, ever. His brothers were splatting hard like calves who'd been lassoed at full gallop in a branding pen, turning into soft, besotted fools. Nathaniel had always been a bit on the sensitive side, but Blake had thought Adam and Travis were tougher than they'd turned out to be. At least Travis had become easier to get along with since he and Dakota had gotten back together and tied the knot, so it wasn't all bad.

But Blake was plenty easygoing already. He didn't need a woman to soften him up. Any mushier, and he'd be a bowl of quivering jelly, not a brawny cowboy.

"Are you even listening to me?" Felicity clenched his fisted shirt a little tighter.

"Uh, yeah. Sure."

Disgust curled her lip. "I can't think what I ever saw in you."

"Hey, now. I'm a hot cowboy. Pretty sure those were your words." He bobbed his eyebrows.

Felicity shook her head and snorted a short laugh. "I take them back. Get out of my life, and don't come anywhere near my friends, either. I'll warn them."

Blake studied her for a few seconds. "Why, Felicity, darling, I think you started to care for me. Otherwise, our agreement should have been fine."

Her eyebrows tipped up. "In your dreams, cowboy." She pivoted on her three-inch heels and strode away.

Blake watched her hips sway in her short skirt as she marched down the sidewalk. He rubbed the back of his neck. All that fuss because she'd learned he'd asked Marnie Wilson to go to a Kenny Chesney concert in Missoula with him on the weekend. Felicity didn't even like country music, so what was the big deal? He'd always insisted on a non-exclusive relationship. It was on her if that started bugging her six months later.

Just meant she found him irresistible. A little grin quirked at the corners of his mouth. That was him, Blake the heartbreaker. Get serious? Not a chance.

He only had to look at his dad to realize what intentional Cavanagh relationships looked like. His parents had yelled and cussed and thrown things at each other for years, only ending when Mom stalked out just before Blake's tenth birthday.

Good riddance. Dad may still have had a volatile temper and been hard to please, but the huge house had been a lot quieter. Not that Blake and his brothers had stayed inside much. No way. They were wild creatures jumping on any horse in the corral and galloping off bareback. Except Dad's mount. That would have gotten them a tanning for sure.

And then Dad met Kathryn Anderson, married the poor widow, adopted her three sons, and been a mostly nice guy for a couple of years, during which time Kathryn homeschooled the entire tribe of boys and gave birth to twin girls.

The honeymoon hadn't lasted long. Dad started bellowing again, and Kathryn withdrew. She was hardier than Mom had ever been, retreating to a suite of rooms in the walk-out basement and sticking it out until just last week.

The revelation Dad had another daughter barely older than the twins had been the straw that broke the figurative camel's back. Mom moved to town with the girls and got a job teaching English at Creekside Academy.

Dad was beside himself, pacing the quiet house at all hours, riding out on Diesel in the middle of the night, snarling at any of the boys who came within ten feet of him.

A fool for love? Or maybe just a fool.

Yeah, Blake wasn't gonna be that guy. He didn't have Dad's temper — thank the good Lord for that — but he'd seen it in his brother Travis. Whatever Dad and Travis did, Blake was on the opposite trail. Not him. No way.

He adjusted his cowboy hat on his head and looked past the line of trees marking the edge of the beach along Jewel Lake. He took a deep breath. Okay. Felicity was gone. There were other women. Arlene was still ready for a good time, and then there was Marnie.

Marnie! He was supposed to meet her at the Copper Carafe ten minutes ago, but he'd run into Felicity after he'd parked the truck beside the town square. Dagnabbit, women hated when he was late.

Blake glanced both ways before angling across the street toward the coffee shop then paused for a second to make sure his plaid shirt was neatly tucked in, exposing his gleaming belt buckle. Women loved the thing. Mark of a macho cowboy or something like that.

He pulled open the door and scanned the busy place. Many of the tables were surrounded by groups, and at least half a dozen people stood in line.

Ah. There she was, standing with her back to Blake as she looked down. On her phone, maybe? He hadn't seen that outfit on her before — she was usually in jeans or shorts — but it was cute. Knee-length gray skirt, low heels, a soft pink top with fluttery sleeves. Her dark hair was held in a bun with pencils, and he grinned at the schoolmarm look.

She hadn't seen him yet. This could be fun. Blake sidled closer to the line, intent on his prey, but she didn't look up. He stopped right behind her, breathing in the fragrance of the coffee shop and... lilacs? He held back a chuckle. Marnie was full of surprises today.

In one swift move, he pulled the pencils holding her hair together. His arms came around her from behind as he nuzzled into the crook of her neck.

Oof!

Blake gasped for breath as her elbow jammed hard into his solar plexus. Before he could blink, she dropped into a crouch, grabbed behind his knees, hooked her foot behind his, and pushed.

Flat on his back, he blinked up at the woman. She was very much not Marnie.

Dafne Santoro stared at the man sprawled on the ceramic tile floor. Shock covered his face as he gawked back.

The guy was kind of cute, not that it mattered. He wore a plaid shirt and well-worn jeans held in place by a leather belt and a buckle that had to be all for show. Cowboy boots on his feet confirmed she wasn't in Spokane anymore.

"You're not Marnie!" His voice rang with accusation.

She blinked. "Pardon me?"

"I thought you were someone else." He struggled to sit up then reached for the brown cowboy hat laying a few feet away. He rubbed the back of his skull, still glaring at her, then clapped on the hat as he surged to his feet. "That hurt."

Dafne backed up a step to keep some distance. "I'm sorry?" But she wasn't. Not really. Who expected to be accosted in line at a coffee shop? Not her, for one.

People around them were staring. A few were snickering. She probably looked a disaster with her hair tumbled around her shoulders. She straightened her skirt and held out her hand. "I'll take my pencils back now, please."

The man's eyes glimmered. "I'm not so sure about that."

A woman with long dark hair marched up to the guy and, before he could blink, shoved him backward. "You're a womanizing jerk, Blake the snake. I'm done." And she sashayed toward the door in her snug tank top and short shorts.

"Marnie!" he called. "Wait a minute. I can explain."

Snickers surrounded them, silenced only when the cowboy — Blake? — pivoted to glare at the coffee crowd.

"Miss? I'm ready to take your order."

If there was anything Dafne hated, it was being the center of attention. It was bad enough when it was for an award, like graduating at the top of her class at Gonzaga U. It was ten times worse when she'd done something public and stupid in a town she hoped to make her home. She tucked her long hair behind her ears.

"I, uh… just a coffee, please. Black." She'd meant to get a macchiato or something like her friends back home always ordered. As a single mom all through college, every penny she could spare had gone to keeping Gavin fed and clothed. Yes, her parents had helped a lot, but her six-year-old wasn't the result of *their* mistakes. He was her responsibility, not theirs.

"We'll share one of those doughnuts, too." Blake's breath warmed her cheek, he was that close. Had he not learned anything in the past few minutes?

Dafne held out her debit card, but his hand extended past hers holding his. "I've got it."

"No, thank you."

"I insist."

She let out a frustrated breath as the server took the cowboy's card instead of hers, the girl's eyelashes batting at the man. Dafne wouldn't make more of a scene, but seriously! Who did he think he was? He'd already made a spectacle out of her, and she'd thank him to walk away and let the townsfolk think about something else for a while.

Dafne gritted her teeth. "Thank you." Dad would be disappointed if he heard she'd been this rude. Let alone that she'd dropped a guy to the floor. Of course, it was Dad who'd enrolled her in jiu jitsu long before she became pregnant with Gavin. She should have used it on Connor Hamelin instead of letting him into her life.

Dafne really, really hated men who thought they were God's gift to women.

And she needed to stop woolgathering, because Blake now had two coffees and a plated doughnut on a tray. "Where would you like to sit?"

She reached for a mug. "Anywhere without you."

He chuckled as he twisted slightly to keep the tray out of reach. "Not happening. How about over there?" His chin poked toward a table just being vacated by a pair of middle-aged women.

Three choices. Shut up and sit down. Walk out without her coffee… or throw it at him. But people still eyed them curiously, and she didn't need to be the talk of the town.

The new social sciences teacher made such a scene in the Copper Carafe! You should have seen it. You could excuse her dropping the cowboy on his rear for sneaking up on her, but then she threw her coffee cup at him! Whisper, whisper.

Besides, she needed that caffeine. She'd dropped Gavin off at the academy-run daycare and had less than an hour before staff orientation with Ms. Cantrell.

Dafne raised her chin. She wasn't going to let this cowboy intimidate her or walk all over her. But she *had* dumped him. She could kind of understand his desire to save a little face after his meeting with the concrete floor. After all, this was probably his hometown, so he was likely known by many of the onlookers. And Marnie, who'd apparently been his girlfriend, had broken up with him rather publicly. "Fine."

Blake flashed her a grin. "You won't regret it."

Her eyebrows shot up. "Know what I hate?"

He set the tray on the table. "What?"

"Men who think they know what's best for a woman they just met. Because, guess what? You don't. For all you know, I'm happily married with five kids." She tucked her hands behind her back lest he see her ringless fingers.

"Five kids?" His eyebrows shot up. "You're all of twenty-one."

"Twenty-three. And it could be true. A couple of sets of twins, and bam."

Blake chuckled and held out a chair for her, gesturing for her to take a seat.

She sat primly on the edge. "May I have my pencils back now, please?"

He pulled them from his hip pocket and laid them on the table between them. "Sure. And I'm betting no to five kids."

Dafne tucked the pencils in her crossbody bag then reached for the white ceramic bowl stuffed with packets of sweetener. She dumped the contents of three into her mug.

"I could have told you you needed a bit more sweetening," he drawled.

"Do you insult every woman you meet?" She glanced at him as she stirred the coffee.

"Do you flatten every guy you meet?"

She narrowed her gaze. "There's a first for everything."

"Ditto."

Somehow, she didn't believe him. The provocations came too easily from his lips for this to be an unusual occurrence.

He nudged the doughnut plate closer to her side of the table. "This is yours."

"I didn't order it." But it smelled yeasty and sugary and heavenly, and she'd only had a superfood smoothie before driving Gavin to daycare. Of course, she'd made sure he had an egg and toast before his big day. She simply hadn't been able to stomach the thought for herself.

"I ordered it for you. Unless you're celiac, you should just say 'thank you' and then eat it."

It did smell tempting. Her resistance faded. "Thank you." The first bite melted in her mouth. Not as good as the cinnamon buns at the bistro back home, but pretty good.

"How about going out with me Saturday night? I have two tickets to see Kenny Chesney in Missoula."

Dafne choked and barely managed to get the suddenly dry morsel down before she surged to her feet. "No."

And she walked out, leaving that precious coffee behind. And her dignity.

CHAPTER TWO

N ice one, bro."

Blake grimaced as his stepbrother dropped into the newly vacated seat. "Hey." Of all the people to witness his humiliation, it would be Noah, the guy with the strongest code of honor of all the Cavanagh brothers. Noah had been known to rescue stray kittens. He'd never inflict drama on any human being, especially a woman.

Noah slid the abandoned coffee cup out of the way and set his own down. "When are you going to learn?"

"I don't see how it's any of your business what I do and what I don't."

"Probably true. But the Cavanagh name—"

"Don't preach to me about the name I was born with and that you didn't get until you were eleven. The name my father has already wrecked in this town." Word had been seeping out about Dad's long-ago affair that had taken place between his divorce and remarriage. The affair that had resulted in a daughter Dad hadn't publicly acknowledged until Vivienne showed up in town a few weeks back.

"I never figured you for using your dad as an excuse for poor behavior."

Blake's eyes narrowed. "Why are you even sitting here talking to me?"

Noah shrugged. "You looked like you needed a friend."

"Friends don't jab when the other guy is down." Blake's tailbone might never be the same.

"Friends hold each other accountable."

"Puh-leeze."

"I'm not the enemy here."

"Well, you're sure not a friend."

Noah winced. "Bro, the only one you're hurting on this path you're on is you. Although Marnie might have been a little miffed, too."

"I doubt it. She enjoyed that far too much." Blake took a deep breath. "I thought that was her in the line."

"I figured. Honest mistake from the back."

He relaxed a little. "That's what I thought."

"Except for the clothes. And the darker hair. And the fact this woman looked to be several inches shorter."

"Anything else, Mr. Observant?"

Noah's eyes glittered in amusement. "You should have seen the look on your face. I haven't seen you that stunned since that time Incognito bucked you off."

He'd been twelve. "Quit insulting me."

"You make it far too easy. But seriously, Blake, start thinking for just a few seconds before you act? Also, you may not be aware, but there's an entire future to plan for, not just the next hot date."

There was nothing wrong with living in the here and now. But Blake knew better than to say that out loud, especially to Noah, who'd begun apprenticing as a farrier as soon as he had his driver's license then bought out his mentor's mobile horseshoeing business before he turned twenty-three.

He met Noah's gaze. "Fine. You have a point."

The other guy's eyebrows tipped up. "Who was she, anyway?"

"How should I know? We hadn't gotten that far."

"You asked her to a concert without even knowing her name?"

"Whatever." Blake snorted. "She's not my type. Too prim."

"That martial arts takedown isn't what I'd call prim. She's got moves."

His butt still hurt. "So, she's prim and feisty." He eyed his stepbrother. "A goody-goody like her is more what *you're* after." Except she lacked that woebegone puppy look.

"Not looking for a relationship."

"Me, neither." It wasn't often the two of them saw eye to eye.

"Nathaniel seems happy."

Wait. Did Noah sound wistful? "Nat's a sap."

"True that." Noah chuckled.

Huh. "Have they set a date?" Anything to change the subject. Even discussing weddings.

"Beginning of Christmas break."

"Guess you'll be best man."

Noah nodded.

Well, that was legit. The guys were twins, after all. And

it should come as no surprise that Blake was the last to know, since he and Nathaniel weren't exactly close. But, still.

Blake downed half his coffee and poked his chin toward the barely nibbled doughnut. "Split that with you?"

"And here I thought you didn't care."

He rolled his eyes, tore it in half, and offered Noah the part without teeth marks on it. He'd kissed her neck, after all. He'd already absorbed whatever vile diseases she carried.

What twenty-three-year-old woman wore lilac perfume? It smelled so old-ladyish. And then there was that whole thing about having five kids. Could that have been true? Surely not.

This he did know. She wasn't anything like Felicity or Arlene or Marnie, and he was down two girlfriends in the space of less than an hour. He'd never professed love and devotion to any one woman, but he had a sneaking suspicion Ms. Prim wasn't a woman who willingly shared.

And the time might come he'd be okay with that. Probably not this week.

"EVERYONE, I'd like you to meet Ms. Dafne Santoro. She's from Spokane and a graduate of Gonzaga University. She's taking over the Social Sciences department for our high-schoolers." Ms. Cantrell nodded at Dafne as the others turned to look at her.

"Welcome to our crew!" A blond woman about her own

age smiled a welcome. "I'm Ainsley Johnson, and I work at the front desk."

"Ms. Johnson is the oil that keeps our entire academy running," Ms. Cantrell said.

The other woman looked down, blushing. "Thank you."

"Also new this term — but no stranger to most of you — is Ms. Kathryn Cavanagh. She's teaching English Lit and Composition. Many of you know her daughters, Alexia and Emma, who are enrolled in tenth grade here this year."

Ms. Cavanagh looked to be in her fifties. She smiled at Dafne then turned back to Ms. Cantrell. "And my step-daughter, Vivienne Johnson, is transferring here as a Senior."

"That must have been quite a shock for you."

"It was." Ms. Cavanagh shared a look with Ms. Johnson.

Dafne had heard all about small towns. Apparently, everyone knew everyone else and was in each other's business. The Spokane neighborhood she'd been raised in was similar, but that might be because her relatives made up a good percentage of Bridgeview's population. She'd have to pay close attention to catch the nuances in her new town.

She was going to miss home, for sure. Her parents and siblings had been shocked speechless when she'd informed them she'd landed a position two states away. Her sister, Ava, who taught music and dance in several Spokane elementary schools, was convinced Dafne was making a huge mistake.

But, Dafne was done being coddled. She'd made the mistake of her life nearly seven years ago with Connor Hamelin. Since then, she'd put her head down, finished high school, and tucked five years of college under her belt.

She needed a surer path to independence than her sister had taken, and one term of substituting all over the city hadn't netted her a secure enough future to take her young son and move out of her parents' basement.

Creekside Academy in Jewel Lake offered her that and more, so here she was. She'd been sidetracked once, and it wouldn't happen again.

Her mind slid back to the insufferable guy who'd accosted her in the coffee lineup this morning. Insufferable... but cute. Self-confident to the point of arrogant. She only had to think of that ostentatious belt buckle to remind herself that Blake whatever-his-last-name-was wasn't the kind of man she wanted to get to know.

Western Montana seemed a whole different world from Eastern Washington for all that the drive took under four hours. She and Gavin could go home any weekend they wanted, but she'd keep that to a minimum. She was absolutely going to fit in here, no matter what it took. Jewel Lake was her future. She'd keep Gavin away from horses, though. She'd heard enough horror stories to know kids could get bucked off and even trampled by such large beasts. So, no horses. And then there was the lake—

"Ms. Santoro? I'd like to take you and Kathryn to see your classrooms now. Everyone else knows where they're going." The receptionist tucked her blond strands behind her ear.

Dafne's face flushed. She had totally zoned out during the last of the administrator's speech. This was *not* how to make a good first impression. She could only hope no one had noticed. She rose, touching the strap of her crossbody bag. Good, it was in place. "Thanks. Um... you can just call me Dafne. I'm not really used to the whole Ms. Santoro thing."

"In front of the students, I'll have to follow protocol, but otherwise, sure. Call me Ainsley." The woman smiled. "And just so you know the score, I'm engaged to Kathryn's son Nathaniel."

Which explained the large rock she'd seen glistening on Ainsley's finger when she swept her hair back. "Congratulations."

"Welcome to Jewel Lake, Dafne." The older woman stepped up beside her. "I'm happy to meet you."

"Thank you. I'm excited to be here." She followed Ainsley out of the staff room and into a hallway lined with lockers.

"Are you married?" Ainsley asked.

Dafne nearly stumbled on the smooth, flat floor. "No." But a little honesty would go a long way if she hoped to make friends. "I do have a young son, though."

"Being a single mom is a tough gig."

Did the other woman actually know anything about it? "It has its challenges, for sure. But Gavin means everything to me, and he's the reason I accepted this position."

"How old is he?" Kathryn asked.

"Just turned six. He'll be starting first grade in the other wing, which is an amazing opportunity for him." Dafne'd steeled her heart against Gavin's tears at moving away from his grandparents and all his second cousins. This was best for them both. It was.

"Just a year older than Nathaniel's nephew, Toby." Ainsley gestured through an open door. "Welcome to your new home away from home. Kathryn, you're right here across the hall."

Dafne stepped inside as the other two women's voices faded. Her own classroom. Several tables, each seating four, formed rows facing the ancient-looking wooden desk.

Her desk. Her very own teacher's desk.

She swallowed hard against the upswell of emotion and blinked back the tears. "Thank You, God," she whispered. "Thank You for taking such good care of me." She didn't deserve it.

No, Ava called that stinkin' thinkin'. No one deserved the good things God bestowed on them. Dafne wasn't any more terrible a human than anyone else just because she'd been a self-absorbed teenager who'd gone her own way and found herself pregnant partway through her Junior year.

Dafne crossed to the large windows and looked out on the parking lot between the academy and its anchor church, Creekside Fellowship. She and Gavin would be there for Sunday school this weekend. Search results revealed a couple of other evangelical assemblies in town, but they'd give this one first try.

The quiet street she'd driven in on ran along one side of the parking lot. Across from it, trees lined a creek that tumbled into the lake a dozen blocks away.

Dafne took a deep breath and turned to face her classroom. A wide shelving unit loaded with books covered the back wall, and yellowed maps adorned the wall against the hallway.

Her classroom.

She'd done it. Not only juggled single parenthood and classes to graduate magna cum laude, but found a job she was uniquely suited for, even if it was far from home. She couldn't have done it without Mom and Dad, but from now on? She was standing on her own two feet. She'd pay them back somehow for all the years of living in their basement and eating their food and accepting their help with Gavin.

"I'm sorry it's all so... ancient." Ainsley's voice came from the doorway. "The desk, the bookshelves, the maps, everything."

"It's okay." And it was. "I teach history, so glass and stainless steel wouldn't seem quite right." But those maps might be several decades out of date.

Ainsley laughed. "You have a point there. I'm really impressed by you. Maybe a little intimidated."

"Me?" Dafne pressed her hand to her heart. "There's nothing extraordinary about me."

"Sure, there is. You're only twenty-three and a full-fledged teacher. I'm four years older with little education and a receptionist job."

"Ms. Cantrell said she couldn't run this place without you."

"She could." Ainsley gave a rueful chuckle. "She mostly has. I've only been back for a month."

That was an odd set of comments. Dafne'd think those through before asking for clarification.

"I lived here for a few months a couple of years ago and worked at the academy. But then I got pregnant..."

Ah, she *did* understand.

Ainsley waved a hand. "Lots of things happened. I went back to Spokane — that's where you're from, too, right?"

"Yes! What part of the city?"

"North Hill."

"I lived in Bridgeview, just west of downtown."

"I've seen it from across the river at Kendall Yards. Anyway, I was in an accident, lost my memory... long story. But my little girl, Bella, and I are glad to be back here."

"And you're engaged."

"Yes, to Bella's dad. Best of all possible outcomes."

Dafne forced a laugh. "That wouldn't be it for me. Gavin's dad isn't someone I ever want to see again. He's given up any rights to see his son, and that's just fine with me."

"I guess not everyone can live the dream."

"This job is my dream. Being able to support Gavin without depending on my parents, that's my dream. I'm not looking for a guy to whisk me away." Especially not someone like the cocky cowboy in the coffee shop. Ugh.

"Well, I hope we can be friends, anyway. Nathaniel is amazing. He has a couple of married brothers and three more who are as single as they come. So, if you change your mind, I can introduce you to one of them."

"Thanks, but no thanks." Dafne swept her hand around the classroom. "What am I allowed to change in here? Because I have a strong need to make this place my own."

CHAPTER THREE

S o, how's the new school year?" Blake pulled away from the academy parking lot with his younger sisters aboard on Friday afternoon.

Alexia bounced a little in the front seat. At least her seatbelt contained her excitement. "Amazing! Even though we still have Mom for English."

Blake laughed. "Well, she does teach there."

"Funny."

He glanced in the rearview mirror. "How about you, Emma?"

"I think I'm going to like it. We know most everyone from church, but there's this new teacher—"

"Ms. Santoro," Alexia interrupted. "She's cool. She needs to loosen up a little, but other than that—"

"I think she just doesn't have a ton of experience," Emma protested. "And keeping a strict classroom might be her thing, regardless."

"Maybe." Alexia shrugged. "I doubt she can make history interesting, but she's welcome to try."

Blake glanced at Alexia as he turned onto the highway toward Rockstead Ranch. "What's wrong with history?"

She rolled her eyes. "Boring. Who cares what the settlers did on the Oregon Trail? Like, seriously."

"Even worse, ancient history like with the Vikings and stuff."

Blake bit back a chuckle. "What's your favorite subject, Emma? Besides not history." Come to think of it, he hadn't been particularly fond of history himself. At least the twins had the chance to attend a real school, unlike him and his brothers. Oh, they'd gone for a couple of years after Mom stormed out — one of Dad's hired hands drove them down from the ranch every morning and picked them up every afternoon — but that had ended with Dad's marriage to Kathryn.

"I'd like English if someone besides Mom taught it."

Alexia wrinkled her nose. "Another boring subject. Give me art or P.E."

"Well, you two need to make the best of your opportunity. After all, you've been nagging to go to regular school for years now, and you finally can."

The girls exchanged a glance. "I didn't mean for it to happen because Mom left Dad, though." Emma frowned. "I wanted to stay living at the ranch and just go to Jewel Lake every day."

"I like living in town." Alexia crossed her arms. "Except I miss riding Domino. That's the first thing I'm going to do when we get home."

A whole weekend with the girls around... but without their mother. Not that Kathryn had been particularly hands-on when they all still lived at Rockstead.

"Me, too. I want to ride Desiree up to the meadow. Nathaniel taught me how to ground-tie her. Do you think she'll still remember?"

"She's a pretty smart mare. I bet she does." Blake angled the truck up the ranch road. "So, neither of you wants to be a teacher when you grow up, huh?"

Alexia shuddered. "Not me, for sure. Not if I'd have to dress up like Ms. Santoro."

"Don't be silly," Emma put in. "She's from the city. She won't wear skinny skirts and tight buns forever."

"Who puts pencils in their bun to hold it in place?" Alexia said with disgust.

Pencils? Blake perked up. "Who's this again?"

"Our new teacher. We told you. I bet she's barely out of college. I don't think she's really ready to fit into life in Jewel Lake."

"And she wears pencils in her bun?"

Alexia eyed him. "Isn't that what I said?"

"I'm just trying to imagine hair like that." But he didn't need to imagine it. Just last Tuesday, he'd pulled pencils from the bun of a young woman he'd never seen around town before. What were the odds there were two of them?

"Dakota sometimes sticks chopsticks in hers," Emma put in reasonably. "It's not that weird."

"Ms. Santoro, huh? What's her first name?"

Alexia narrowed her gaze at him. "Why do you want to know? Getting low on girlfriends?"

He was, rather. "Just curious."

"Our teachers are off limits to you, Blakey."

"Aren't all the rest of them over forty?"

"Yes—"

"So, who cares about them? Mostly married, too, I bet. Why shouldn't I be curious about a young, pretty teacher?" Blake remembered the young woman's bluff. "Is she single? Does she have five kids?"

"Only one, I think." Alexia scrunched her face. "He's a little first-grader."

Mustn't be the woman he'd met, then. She wasn't old enough to have a six-year-old. She'd said she was twenty-three, so she'd have been seventeen when he was born. Oh, well, the thought had been entertaining while it lasted. It wasn't like anything would have come of it, anyway. She'd taken him down in public and wanted nothing to do with him.

Besides, he didn't even want to get to know such a testy, violent woman.

"She was asking if there was a jiu jitsu club in Jewel Lake." Alexia looked at Blake. "What's that?"

"Uh, a form of martial arts, I think. Haven't heard of anyone doing that around here." But it explained his sore tailbone.

Emma's hands flashed in Blake's rearview mirror in some sort of movie-inspired kung-fu chops. "We should learn karate or something."

Alexia scrunched her face.

"Might not be a bad idea." Blake kept his eyes on the ranch road. "That way if some guy starts giving you unwanted attention, you can take him down."

"Somebody should dropkick *you*," muttered Emma.

"Who's to say somebody hasn't?" Although it hadn't been that maneuver, exactly.

Alexia twisted in her seat, gaze full on his face.

Uh oh.

"Was it you?"

"Was what me?" There was no way his kid sister could know. Could she? But plenty of people had been in the Copper Carafe that morning. He hadn't spent a lot of time cataloguing their faces. It wasn't outside the realm of possibility someone had told his sisters.

"Ms. Santoro told our class how useful jiu jitsu was and that Jewel Lake should really have an academy for it. She said she'd already had to use her training once since she came to town."

"I thought it was called a dojo," said Emma. "*School* is an academy."

"Well, that's what she called it. She knows more than we do. Like how to take a guy down." Alexia eyed Blake. "Sounds fun."

"Maybe for the person doing the move. Less fun for the recipient."

"It *was* you."

Why was the ranch road so long? There were three more curves before they got to the top and Blake could end this discussion. "I've never been dropkicked in my life." Which was a true statement. What the newcomer had done to him was different. Ha. Even then he'd thought she had a teacher or librarian look to her.

But she had a school-age kid, which made her a no-go for him. From what he'd seen, single moms tended to be too focused, too serious, to date a guy like him. Probably something to do with all that responsibility he tried to avoid.

Blake liked his life unencumbered. There was plenty of

time for dutiful stuff in the future. He was only twenty-seven. He could milk his status for a few more years before his father began to care... if Dad even noticed then. He was too wound up about Kathryn's defection to pay attention to anything else right now.

He rolled the truck into the ranch yard and parked beside the corrals. Both girls shoved their doors open and jumped out, leaving their backpacks behind.

Emma tore into the stable, but Alexia leaned back into the truck. "Blake?"

"Hmm?"

"Leave our teacher alone."

He wobbled his eyebrows at her. "I've never asked you for permission to date anyone in my life, and I'm not going to start now. Pipsqueak."

She glowered. "Just don't." And she slammed the truck door a whole lot harder than necessary.

Sounded like a challenge.

"You're not coming home for the weekend?"

Dafne hardened her heart against the pleading in her mother's voice. "No, we'll be spending the time getting settled in our new place and meeting our neighbors. Maybe in a couple of weeks, you and Dad could come visit one weekend."

"It's just not the same here without you."

"I know." The words *I'm sorry* hovered on her lips, but she wasn't.

She'd run away with her boyfriend when she'd found

out she was pregnant. Then she'd run *from* Connor when he'd insisted on an abortion. She'd landed up at her cousin's place in Helena. It was Rob and Bren who'd encouraged her to spread her wings now.

Everyone had put their own lives on hold back then to support her. She appreciated it. She did. But it meant her mother hovered, always trying to help, whether Dafne needed it or not.

Maybe not every college graduate felt compelled to move this far from home. Her married siblings both lived within a few blocks of Mom and Dad. But Dafne needed greater separation. She needed to prove to herself as well as to her family that she was, in fact, a grownup now. It was time to take full responsibility for herself and Gavin.

"Maybe." Mom was still sniffling. "I still think—"

Was that a knock? "Mom, someone's at the door. I've got to go, but I'll talk to you later. Or maybe you can Face-Time Gavin before bedtime. He'd love that. Bye!" And she ended the call.

Dafne hurried over to the door and swung it open to find Ainsley on the other side with a toddler in a stroller. "Hi! Come on in."

"I wanted to welcome you to the neighborhood. We're just around the corner in that townhouse over there." Ainsley pointed.

"Oh, that's great! Won't you come in?" Dafne turned back into her rental. "Gavin! Come meet our neighbors."

"If you're sure we're not inconveniencing you. Oh, I almost forgot. I brought you cookies. These are Bella's favorites, and I thought your little boy might like them, too." She handed a small tin to Dafne.

Gavin skidded to a stop beside her in his sock feet. "Hi! What's in there?"

Dafne held the box out of his reach. "Say hi to Ms. Ainsley and her little girl, Bella."

"Hi!" Gavin watched as Ainsley lifted her daughter out of the stroller. "Does she want to play?"

"Wow, I'm not used to bigger kids, especially boys, asking to play with her." Ainsley set the girl just inside the door, and she toddled off after Gavin. "Fair warning, though. She gets into everything."

"Gavin's used to having lots of kids of various ages around, and he misses that." Dafne closed the door behind her neighbor. Dare she hope she was already making a friend? Sure, Ainsley was a few years older, but that didn't matter.

She did a quick scan of the area for baby-proofing and closed the doors to her bedroom and the bathroom. Gavin's Lego collection was on a shelf out of Bella's reach. She returned to the open kitchen. "Would you like a cup of tea?"

"Sounds lovely, thanks."

Dafne poured water in the kettle and set it to heat. "I'm so glad you came over. My mom was on the phone trying to come to terms with the fact I wasn't coming back to Spokane for the weekend."

Ainsley smiled. "This and every weekend?"

"That's what I'm afraid of. I get that it's hard to let go of a child, but she doesn't seem to realize I need to make my own way now that I can. It's not that I don't appreciate everything she and Dad have done for me — and it's been a lot — but it seems the best way to say *thank you* is to let them resume their lives the way they would have by now, if I hadn't been their problem child."

"Must be nice to have parents who care." Ainsley gave a soft smile. "I never knew my dad, and my mom passed away last spring, leaving more questions than answers."

"Oh, I'm so sorry to hear that." There Dafne went again, sticking her foot in her mouth, making it sound like she was the only one with problems. That having parents who cared too much was such a terrible hardship.

"It's a long story, but at least through it all I found Nathaniel again." The other woman twisted the diamond ring on her left hand. "And isn't his mom a sweetheart? She's such a good teacher, too. Creekside Academy is lucky to have her on staff. And you, too, of course."

Dafne had bumped into Kathryn Cavanagh a few times over this first week of school, since their classrooms were across the hall. "She does seem nice. Emma and Alexia are her daughters, right?"

Ainsley nodded. "It's been really hard for her. She and her husband separated only a few weeks ago. She's been so brave forging out on her own after years of isolation at their ranch." She hesitated. "It will be a strange weekend for her, since the twins have gone to visit their dad for the first time since the split."

At least Dafne hadn't ever worried about her parents falling out of love. It had happened to a few of her friends over the years, but not hers. "I'm sorry. It must be hard for the girls. For everyone." She'd have to cut them some slack in class. Or maybe not.

"I can't help but feel a little responsible." Ainsley sighed. "If I hadn't brought my sister Vivienne to Jewel Lake to search for answers, we might never have discovered the Cavanagh twins' father was also Vivienne's. So, it seems a little like my fault…"

Dafne stared at her new friend. "Uh, no? It had nothing to do with you, or at least it sure doesn't sound like it."

"I'm good at feeling guilty."

"Well, don't. If you think she'd like something to do, let's invite Kathryn over to watch a movie or have a craft night or something tomorrow. Your place or mine?"

"Oh… Nathaniel…."

"Right, I forgot your fiancé."

"We've got plans Saturday night, but I'm sure Kathryn would love an excuse to get out. It sounds like a fun idea."

And just how was it, again, that Dafne had offered to befriend a woman thirty-some years her senior?

CHAPTER FOUR

W e should plan a retreat up at the ranch with the high-schoolers." Kathryn sat on Dafne's second-hand sofa and curled her feet under her. "Priscilla — Ms. Cantrell — said they usually have a getaway for the older kids, but that the teachers who used to do the organizing are the ones who've left."

"The ones we've replaced?" Dafne reached in the popcorn bowl and helped herself to a handful. She'd tucked Gavin in bed twenty minutes ago, and he'd finally quit coming out for a drink or a pit stop.

"Yes. It's supposed to be some kind of team-building exercise. Or trust-building, which I guess is the same thing."

"I don't know anything about ranches," Dafne confessed. "Give me an urban escape room, and I can show you a team-building exercise."

"I've heard of those. I think there are a couple in Missoula. But the school board is thinking more of a weekend retreat with devotionals and outdoor skills and quiet time. That sort of thing."

"I can't help. The only outdoor skill I have is picking tomatoes in my nonna's garden."

"I'm not very outdoorsy either, for all I've lived on a ranch most of my adult life. I do like gardening, but mostly flowers." Kathryn looked wistful. "Is it terrible that what I miss the most now is the garden oasis I'd created at Rockstead over the years?"

"Ainsley mentioned you were recently divorced."

"Separated. I'm hoping it doesn't come to divorce, even though I'm the one who left. I'm sorry. I shouldn't be dumping all this on your young shoulders, though I hazard a guess you've experienced more than many women your age."

"I brought it on myself. But you know, I wouldn't trade Gavin for anything."

"Is his dad in the picture?"

Dafne shook her head. "Not really. He sends money when he can, but he's kind of drifting. Last I heard he was working on a truck farm in Kansas."

"Do you think you might get back with him?"

"I really don't see it. He was a self-centered jerk in high school, and I can't say he's improved a whole lot. Mind you, he doesn't know the Lord, and he had the most dysfunctional family I ever met."

"I wonder if it could be worse than the Cavanaghs." Kathryn pursed her lips and shook her head. "Couples who aren't on the same page, spiritually and otherwise, can have a very hard go of it."

"I've seen that. And it's why I'm pretty determined to

make my own way. With God's help, of course, but I don't need a man in my life."

"I should have had more of that attitude when my husband passed away, leaving me with three young boys. My recently divorced brother-in-law was pressuring me to marry him — he wanted the ranch Joe and I owned — and in the end, I took Declan Cavanagh's offer, partly to slam the door in Jason's face."

See? Other people had faced bigger obstacles than Dafne. Kathryn had been widowed, remarried, and was now separated. But that just firmed up Dafne's thoughts on staying single. It was much safer for both her and her son to navigate life without the risk of letting someone unfaithful in. Teaching was perfect, at least now that she'd been hired by this private school. Her time off would coincide with Gavin's, simplifying their life immensely.

"Will you help me plan a high-school retreat then?"

Dafne blinked. Hadn't she just told the older woman that she was not at all outdoorsy? "I can't..."

"I meant just the planning parts. Although you might enjoy the camping part, too, if you've never done it before. But I can get one of my boys to provide some hands-on help as needed."

Her boys? Ainsley had mentioned something about her fiancé's single brothers. Uh, nope. No one was setting Dafne up.

Kathryn laughed. "I can see by your face what you think I meant. No, my eldest, Adam, is happily married, and Nathaniel is engaged to Ainsley. That just leaves Nat's twin, Noah, but he works out of town too much to be of any help with this project."

"Whew." Dafne sagged against the back of the sofa with a dramatic flair.

"On the other hand, two of my stepsons are still single, but I doubt either of them would suit you. I'm not the kind to meddle in the ways of romance, anyway. Not after the fiasco of the past few years with Declan."

"You no longer believe in love." Dafne knew she liked Kathryn. They were kindred spirits.

"That's not what I meant at all. I do believe in love. God loved us so very much that, while we were still sinners, He sent His Son to die for us. Without love of that magnitude, the world ceases to rotate."

"Right, but that's different from romantic love."

"It is, and it isn't."

Dafne raised her eyebrows.

"Paul likens marriage to God's relationship with the church. I think love is love, and experiencing it in one facet of our lives can only help it to grow and mature in other areas, too."

"But you're separated." Which Dafne should not have said out loud.

"You're right, but it's not because I don't believe in love. I believe Declan needs to fall in love with Jesus, and so do I. Oh, I've attended church most of my life, and dragged my kids along. But it had become rote. I believed because it was more comfortable to keep believing. I kept reading my Bible and devotional books because it was a habit that seemed worth continuing, even though it felt dry and lifeless."

Best to choose her words carefully. "I can see how it could become that."

Kathryn spun her wedding rings on her finger. She might not even realize she was doing it, not with that faraway look in her eyes. Finally, she focused on Dafne with a halfhearted chuckle. "You and me, girl, we've made some poor choices, but God's in the redemption business. Now that I'm living away from Declan and the ranch, I'm hoping to think more clearly. Praying for that. I don't know how God will answer my prayers, and honestly, it's hard to trust Him for it. But I have to believe, based on His word, that He has a purpose in everything. My part is to wait patiently and expectantly."

Dafne fidgeted. How had this conversation turned so deep? She didn't even know this woman, not really, but now she knew her life story and deepest spiritual struggles.

"I'm sorry, Dafne. I've made you uncomfortable."

Great. She needed to learn to school her reactions. She managed a smile. "If you can promise I won't get a mosquito bite or have to sleep in a tent, I'll try to help you plan this event. But it's up to you. I'm only the assistant."

Kathryn smiled. "I can make no promises, but mosquitoes are nearly done for the season, and I'm pretty sure the boys have mattress pads to soften the hard ground, even though they rarely even admit to tents in the high country."

No tents? No mattresses? Dafne was so not up for a camping trip. She was a city girl, through and through. "I can help with planning. And, if I can bring Gavin, maybe a day trip to oversee an activity or two. That's all I'm comfortable with."

"I'll take that for now."

BLAKE OPENED the truck door for Arlene Saturday evening. "I hope you enjoyed the concert."

She batted her eyes at him as she clambered in. "It wasn't too terrible, cowboy."

Yeah, she hadn't claimed to be a country music fan, but he'd been out of datable women to invite. Blake rounded the vehicle and climbed in. When he reached to insert the key in the ignition, she rested her hand on his forearm. He stilled, tilting his eyebrows at her.

"We should go to a club. Or maybe back to my place."

Blake studied her for a few seconds. Her extra-long eyelashes fluttered in a face so made-up he almost wondered what she actually looked like.

Arlene's fingers slid up and down his arm, the flecks in her nail polish glistening in the dim light of the cab.

What was he doing with her? She was no improvement over Felicity or Marnie. All she wanted was to get him in her bed. And he was tired of the games. Which was ridiculous, because hadn't he just told himself everything he had in common with Peter Pan? No growing up for Blake Daniel Cavanagh. Life was short enough as it was. A guy might as well milk the years he was young.

"Not tonight." He gave her a grin meant to soften the words.

Her gaze narrowed as her thin eyebrows hiked. "And here I thought you'd be ready for a really good time. Since I finally have you to myself."

Why, again, had he thought juggling three women was a good idea? Just as puzzling, why did he suddenly think it was stupid? He started the truck. "You heard, huh?"

"Felicity told me she got tired of your games. And the

town grapevine has been busy about what happened in the Copper Carafe. How you kissed some stranger's neck thinking she was Marnie, and then Marnie belted you and broke up with you." Arlene let out a little giggle.

"And you still said yes to tonight?" He maneuvered the truck through the parking lot.

"Sure. What woman likes to share?"

Uh. "Didn't bother you before."

He caught her headshake in his peripheral vision. "I'm sure we all thought we'd be the one to win over the others."

Like he was a prize buckle in a rodeo event, played out on live television. Maybe the analogy wasn't too far off.

That teacher, though. She'd never toy around. She'd be playing for keeps from the start. Though, she did have a kid with no father-figure in sight according to his sisters. Never mind. She'd totally rejected the game by dropping him to the unforgiving floor in public.

Which Blake's present company found amusing.

There was something wrong with this picture. And the fact he recognized it was even more troubling. Where was the bubble he loved to live in so much? The one that reminded him of perpetual youth and lack of commitment?

Blake wanted his bubble back. Because if it began to disintegrate, who knew where that might lead? He didn't want to find out. Accepting maturity was a trap from which he'd never escape.

"Blake?" Arlene's voice was edged with impatience. "If you don't want to, just say so. No need to get all sulky."

Sulky? He'd show her sulky. Or not. She wasn't worth

the bother. And if that were true, tonight was their last date.

Panic threatened to overcome him. How had he gone from three girlfriends to none in five short days? And with very little desire to go through the effort of replenishing the stock? He hadn't been solo since high school. Who even was he without a woman hanging onto his arm?

Blake turned onto the main thoroughfare before glancing at Arlene, who sat with her arms crossed. "You're right."

Her eyebrows tilted up again. "About what? Do I want to know?"

"We're not going to work."

"Sure, we will. We can be exclusive without getting serious, cowboy."

Sounded like a slippery slope to him. Why be exclusive if he didn't want to marry the woman? Also, why did he react so negatively at the thought of marrying Arlene or anyone else? He didn't want to. He didn't want to settle down.

But he didn't want to carry on like this, either.

Blake shook his head. "I don't think we can. Sorry." Yet, not sorry.

Arlene uttered an incredulous laugh. "Is this just so you can say you ended a relationship yourself instead of the girl doing it?"

Was ego all that urged him on? Maybe, but he didn't think so. Blake shrugged. "Don't know." He also didn't know what he was going to do about it all. Seek out another girlfriend or two or three? Not in Jewel Lake. It wasn't big enough for his reputation. A reputation he'd quite enjoyed only a few weeks — a few days — ago.

He navigated out onto the interstate toward Jewel Lake. Was there anything left to say to Arlene? He couldn't think of it.

"Don't bother trying to crawl back," she announced from the other side of the cab.

"I won't."

"I'm done with you."

"I understand." It went both ways.

Arlene huffed a laugh. "I can't believe this. I was certain I'd be the one to turn you around."

His blood chilled. Now he'd only been a challenge? Great. Another blow for his ego. *Ego's not everything.* And while that was true, it was still something. It might be everything he'd had.

Pitiful.

He didn't even want to think about how pathetic that was. Even his fifteen-year-old sisters had recognized it.

A woman like their new teacher would never stoop to someone like him. She might be young, and she might have a kid, but she had loftier goals than a guy like Blake. Seemed like she had enough determination to succeed at them, too.

She'd probably forgotten all about him by now, though maybe not. How many guys did she dump on the floor in a week?

Maybe she remembered him.

But it wouldn't be fondly.

CHAPTER FIVE

"Class dismissed."

It was amazing how rapidly the classroom emptied after the final bell on a Friday afternoon. Dafne could hardly believe two weeks had already gone by, and she faced another long, empty weekend when she could, instead, take Gavin back to her parents' home in the Bridgeview neighborhood of Spokane. She could be there before dark and return to Jewel Lake Sunday afternoon. She'd get a visit with her parents and Nonna. She'd see her brother, Peter, and his wife, Sadie. She'd hang out with her sister, Ava, her husband, Seth, and their kids. Gavin adored little Leo. He adored all his second cousins, too.

Why was she so stubborn about not returning home?

Dafne gathered her folders of pop quizzes to mark over the weekend, remembering Alexia Cavanagh's groan earlier in the day. The grading would only take a couple of hours.

Should she change her mind and make everyone else

happy, especially Gavin and Mom? Was she simply being stubborn, or was it actually important to loosen those apron strings if not cut them completely?

Dafne straightened out a few chairs before looking around her classroom. Folders tucked under her arm, she flipped off the bank of light switches and stepped into the hallway.

Kathryn glanced up from her desk in the other classroom and smiled. "Heading out already?"

"Yes, Gavin is likely waiting for me."

"Good for you."

Still, Dafne hesitated. "How about you? Are the twins going to the ranch this weekend?"

Kathryn shook her head. "They've invited Vivienne over tonight. She's in one of your classes, isn't she?"

"History and Social Studies both. She's an eager student."

The older woman chuckled. "That's not something you can say about Emma and Alexia. Having other teens around is still pretty distracting to them."

"I hear you homeschooled them until this year?"

"Yes. They'll settle in. At least, I hope so."

Vivienne was Ainsley's sister. And if Viv was spending the weekend with the Cavanagh twins, might that mean Ainsley would welcome some single-mom time? Dafne hesitated to ask. Ainsley had a fiancé and a wedding to plan, after all. She wasn't rattling around on weekends with no purpose.

Couldn't hurt to feel out the situation, though. Right?

Dafne checked her watch. It would only take a minute, and it wasn't like it was a big deal if someone had already walked Gavin over to the daycare room. This was definitely one of the best perks to her position, not that she wanted to take advantage of it.

She waved goodbye to Kathryn and made her way down the wide staircase to the academy's main level.

Ainsley glanced up from her spot behind the counter with a smile. "Heading out, Ms. Santoro?"

Man, that still sounded weird, especially coming from someone older than her. "I am, but I was wondering if you had any free time over the weekend?" Might as well leave it open. "Maybe you'd like to get together sometime."

Her new friend's face brightened. "I'd love that! I often feel at loose ends when Viv has a busy weekend planned."

"But… Nathaniel?"

"He works Monday through Saturday, but this weekend he also has the basic chores on Sunday. The brothers rotate that duty."

Dafne had no clue what kind of chores those might be. She'd never given five seconds' thought to what ranching entailed. "So, he's busy all weekend?"

"I thought I'd take Bella up Saturday afternoon for a picnic, and then she can see her daddy for a bit. You and Gavin should come, too. I bet he'd love it."

So much no. Dafne shook her head as she backed up.

Ainsley grinned. "You've never been riding, have you?"

"No. Horses are huge and dangerous."

"Many of them are big, I'll grant you that. But there are plenty who are the sweetest, most docile creatures you'll ever meet. Please come. I'd love someone to ride with who wasn't born in the saddle."

"Born in the—?"

"Just an expression. Adam's wife, Riley, rides like she's glued to the horse. She's a natural. And Travis's wife, Dakota, has been riding her whole life." Ainsley's eyes grew wide. "Has Gavin met Toby yet? Dakota and Travis's son? They're about the same age, and I bet Toby would love to show Gavin around."

"Um, no, I don't remember that name. And it's okay." Dafne lifted her folders. "I've got quite a bit of grading to do this weekend, actually."

Ainsley laughed. "You obviously need to come and get over your fear."

"I'm not afraid." Much.

"Prove it."

Dafne let out a nervous chuckle. "What is this, junior high? I don't need to prove anything to you or anyone else."

"You're right." Ainsley settled back into her office chair. "On the other hand, I was pretty nervous the first time I rode, but now I truly love it. There's just something so amazing about all that controlled power beneath you. Experiencing nature from an entirely new perspective."

"That's nice."

"Come with me, just this once? I promise if you hate it, I'll never ask again."

It wasn't as though Dafne didn't want to try new things, and she *had* taken a job far from home in a ranching community. Didn't that already make her brave and adventurous? Sort of.

But horseback riding? With someone else who sounded like a beginner? On the one hand, if Ainsley was this confident, it should be okay. On the other hand, would Ainsley know what to do if Dafne got thrown off? She remem-

44

bered watching rodeo on TV for a few minutes once before Dad flipped the channel. The cowboys rode on wildly bucking horses until they landed in the dust. Time after time. It looked painful, though the cowboys rolled to their feet right afterward.

"I'll pick you and Gavin up about two o'clock tomorrow?"

Dafne focused back on Ainsley's wistful face, and her determination wavered. "You're sure it's safe?"

Ainsley crossed her heart. "Promise. And Gavin will love it. I'll check with Dakota to see if Toby can come, too."

Gavin needed a friend outside of school. Maybe not a cowboy kid, though... but Ainsley was right. Dafne couldn't keep her son — or herself — bubble-wrapped forever. She could try, but deep inside, she knew better.

She sighed. "Okay. What should I wear?"

"Jeans. Comfy clothes. I don't imagine you have cowboy boots?"

"Why would I?"

Ainsley laughed. "Good point."

"I can just wear my runners, can't I?"

"They'll do in a pinch, but cowboy boots are the right shape to fit in stirrups."

And here Dafne had thought they were just for swagger.

She took a deep breath. What was she getting in for?

BLAKE CLIPPED lead lines to the halters on his sisters' horses. He'd pony them behind Zorro so they could get some exercise. This was the big problem with the girls living in town now and not even coming home every weekend. The horses could get away with being unridden for a few days, but not the better part of two weeks.

And it wasn't like he had anything better to do. He hadn't had a night out since last weekend's ill-fated date with Arlene. Also, he had no prospects in sight, which gave him a restless feeling in his gut. He didn't want to think about it too much, but was there some deep-seated reason he couldn't settle... and that no respectable woman would go out with him?

Like the schoolteacher. Dropping him had been sheer reflex on her part, for which he could scarcely blame her. It seemed symbolic somehow, though, which he didn't want to think too deeply about.

"Woolgathering again?" Blake's father's harsh voice came from behind him.

"Checking the bridles."

"Hmph."

Blake glanced over his shoulder as he fingered Domino's mane. "Doing okay?"

"Why wouldn't I be?"

"Just asking."

"You just do your chores, and don't worry about anything else."

"Yes, sir." Had anyone had a civil conversation with Dad since Kathryn left a few weeks ago? Blake could pick from either of his brothers or even his stepbrothers if he needed a sounding board, but who did Dad have? His Sunday morning coffee buddies at the Copper Carafe, but Blake doubted his father discussed his marital difficulties with any of the other area ranchers. They likely talked about the weather and the price of cattle and who'd purchased a new bull.

The sound of an approaching vehicle caught Blake's attention as he led the two mares out into the corral where Zorro was waiting. He shoved his hat back on his head a bit as he turned to see who was coming. Rockstead was a solid half-hour drive from town. People didn't randomly drive by for the fun of it.

Blue Honda. That would be Nathaniel's fiancée and their daughter.

Blake swung up into Zorro's saddle, aware his father still stood with his hands on his hips, staring at the car. Dad wasn't going to start something with Ainsley, was he? The man was going around like the slightest flicker could spark an explosion. Maybe Blake should hang around a minute longer and make sure nothing happened.

Someone was in the front passenger seat — someone with dark hair, not blond like Ainsley's sister — Dad's daughter — Vivienne. Blake dared breathe. Dad hadn't figured out how to talk nicely to Viv yet. For that matter, neither had Blake, for all Vivienne was apparently his sister as much as Alexia and Emma were. Thing was, he'd known the twins since birth. Vivienne was the newcomer to their messy family.

But who was with Ainsley if not her sister? Blake narrowed his gaze. Flowing locks that looked a lot like the hair of someone whose pencil-secured bun had just been pulled apart. And that pretty face triggered the rest of Blake's memory.

No way was she Ainsley's friend. Yet hadn't he figured

out the woman had to be the twins' new teacher? And Ainsley worked at Creekside Academy, so it made sense.

At least he was on his home turf this time around. He should just nudge Zorro into motion and canter away, so she could see what a real cowboy looked like in his element.

Nah, that was dumb. He could impress her more by hanging around and proving he was a normal human being who didn't make a habit of sneaking up behind women and kissing their necks.

He still couldn't believe he'd done that. That he hadn't realized the subtle differences between this woman and Marnie even without seeing her face. *Thanks for pointing out the obvious, Noah...*

The two women exited the car then each turned to open a backdoor. Ainsley lifted Bella from her car seat, but the other woman released two little boys, one of them Toby.

Toby's face lit up and he darted toward Blake, stopping just out of reach of the mares' hooves. "Unca Blake!"

"Hey, buddy. I'm glad you remembered not to run at the horses."

"Yeah, I don't wanna get kicked in the face."

The woman's cheeks blanched. Not that Blake was watching. Okay, yes, he was. She clutched the other little boy's hand, but was her pallor because of the horses or because she'd recognized Blake?

He tipped his hat. "Ma'am."

"Um. Hi." Her gaze darted to Ainsley then over to Dad and back to Blake.

"Declan, Blake, I'd like you to meet my friend Dafne

Santoro. She's new to Creekside Academy, teaching history and social sciences. And this is her little boy, Gavin. Dafne, this is Nathaniel's stepdad, Declan, and his stepbrother, Blake."

Dad's chin came up slightly. Probably hated the reminder Creekside Academy existed and had swallowed up his wife and daughters. "Nathaniel's out on the range."

Ainsley smiled. "I know. I was hoping I could get some help saddling up a couple of horses for Dafne and me. She's never been riding."

Dafne. That was her name. Pretty, like her. She didn't look so prissy today, wearing artfully ripped jeans — ridiculous as that was — and a gray T-shirt sporting a Gonzaga Bulldogs logo.

The little boy — Gavin? — danced at her side, pointing at the horses. The kid was obviously a little more into this visit than his mother. Though Dafne might have thought it was great before she recognized him.

Blake swung off Zorro and dropped the reins. The gelding wouldn't go anywhere, and the mares' leads were still looped on the corral posts. "I'd be happy to give you two a hand saddling up. In fact, I was just taking Domino and Desiree out for some exercise. They'd enjoy being ridden instead of ponied behind Zorro. Maybe Dad could get Clover ready."

Dad harrumphed, but he'd do it.

"What about me?" asked the little boy. "Do I get a horse? I never ever rode one before."

As Blake suspected. Bella usually rode up with Ainsley or Nathaniel, but if neither the other woman nor her son had experience, it wasn't a good idea to put them together.

Blake made a snap decision. "You can ride with me, squirt." He patted the leather saddle. "See? There's room for both of us right here."

"Oh. No. That won't be necessary." Dafne took a couple of steps backward, right into the car. "We'll just, uh, wait right here. Gavin and I don't need to ride."

"But, Mama!"

"Oh, he'll be perfectly safe with Blake. That's a great idea. And I've ridden Desiree before, so if you don't mind, Blake? I mean, I hate to take you from your duties…"

"My job this afternoon is exercising horses, so you'd actually be doing me a favor." He darted a glance at Dafne. "It's really no problem, ma'am."

Her back stiffened. Was it from the formal address, or because she was feeling challenged? Looked like riding hadn't been entirely her choice.

"Fine."

Blake resisted the fist pump.

CHAPTER SIX

O nce upon a time, she'd run away from home in the dead of winter. She'd given birth at seventeen. More recently, she'd moved two states away from everything she'd ever known. Surely, Dafne was brave enough to sit on a horse.

The animals stood patiently, heads down, tails swishing while Blake swung a saddle on the back of one of them.

What had the woman in the coffee shop called him before she belted him? *Blake the snake.* Yeah. Dafne hadn't liked him then, and she didn't like him now. How could such an obnoxious womanizer be sweet Ainsley's soon-to-be brother-in-law? And even worse, he assumed Dafne's precious baby would ride with him.

She didn't trust him as far as she could throw him. Come to think of it, she'd already taken him down once. She could do it again if needed, although he'd be on guard now. He wouldn't dare mess with her. Not in front of Ainsley or his dad.

The older man scowled as he exited the stable with a

pony plodding along behind him. He motioned to Toby with his chin. "Get on up."

"Okay! Thanks, Grandfather!" Somehow the little boy, a year younger than Gavin, scrambled into the saddle. The height was lower than the other horses, but still, Dafne couldn't help but be impressed.

The boy leaned forward and wrapped his arms around the pony's neck. "I love you, Clover."

Declan smacked the pony's rump, and it shifted forward, the boy straightening in the saddle.

Meanwhile, Bella, in the arms of her mama, patted one of the horses' noses while Blake saddled it.

Was Dafne really going to do this? Every cell in her body screeched in protest, but still she stood rooted to the grassy area just in front of Ainsley's car.

Gavin looked up at his new friend in awe. "You have your own pony? You're so lucky!"

"I know. Clover is just the best. But soon I'll be tall enough for a big horse, right, Grandfather?"

The man grunted. His gaze raked across Dafne, Ainsley, and the children before he pivoted and stalked away.

Realization sank in. This man was Kathryn's estranged husband. Wow, the man was no Mr. Congeniality. Dafne would have to cut the girls some slack in class. Although, no. Probably all of the kids had something or other they were dealing with at home. She couldn't single out Emma and Alexia, especially when they were trying so hard to fit in. But a little understanding went a long way.

Ainsley passed Bella to Blake then mounted up. Blake handed the little one back to her, and she settled the tot in front of her. Then Blake turned to Dafne. "Ready?"

Dafne shook her head involuntarily and tried to back up, but she was already pressed against the hood of Ainsley's car.

Blake grinned and formed an extra stirrup with his hands. "Let me give you a hand up. Put your left foot here, then push up and swing your right leg over. Grab onto the saddle horn if you need it."

If? That thing was going to be her anchor. Dafne eyed the horse, which seemed to have grown another six inches in the past few seconds.

"You can do it, Mama." Gavin's eyes gleamed with excitement.

You're the one who thought moving to Montana was a good idea. Montana has ranches. Your students all probably ride horseback every single day. You can't chicken out now.

Sure she could. Watch her.

Dafne swallowed hard and took a few steps closer. The horse's tail swished as it turned its head to look at her.

"Let's make it easier." And Blake set both hands on her waist and lifted her straight up.

She grabbed his shoulders and somehow managed to get one leg on the other side of the horse. Then she stared down at the cowboy.

He winked, so close she breathed in his masculine scent mingled with leather. "That wasn't so bad, was it?"

She should let go of him, but wouldn't she fall? No. He'd said something about the saddle horn, that leather knob in front of her. But there was only one. She needed outriggers, but there weren't any. Dafne took a deep breath and yanked her gaze away from Blake's dark eyes.

The saddle horn. She transferred one hand from his

shoulder, then the other, wiggling her bottom over a little to feel more balanced. As if that were even possible.

"Okay?"

Not even a tiny bit. She nodded tightly, terrified even the smallest movement would pitch her to the merciless ground below.

The man's hands still rested on her hips like a seatbelt. But she probably couldn't ride with them there, not that she wanted to. Ride at all, that was.

"I'm going to let go now and get your feet in the stirrups." He looked down and tsked. "You'd be better off in boots. If you're going to ride a lot, you'll want a pair."

She wasn't going to ride a lot. Or again. Ever.

He slid one sneakered foot into the stirrup then rounded the other side and repeated the action. "Keep your heels down."

Dafne hadn't fallen off yet. So far, so good, right? She dared a quick glance around. Gavin stared at her with wide eyes. Ainsley offered a thumbs-up with a grin. Bella smacked the horse's neck and giggled.

"Would you rather I led your horse, or do you want the reins?" Blake stroked the horse's mane.

"You."

He smirked as he bobbed his eyebrows.

She might have had the advantage in the Copper Carafe, but he had it here, in spades. All Dafne needed to do was survive and then never say *yes* to Ainsley again. Easy peasy.

Blake hoisted a delighted Gavin into the saddle then swung up behind him. He made it look so effortless. Maybe that's what happened when you rode a hundred hours a day. He leaned down and said something in Gavin's ear.

Her son — her traitorous son — beamed up at the man Dafne couldn't stand. Blake gathered his reins in his left hand and hers in his right. Wait, that didn't leave him one to hold Gavin.

And then he clicked his tongue, and his horse started into a walk.

A second later, so did hers. Dafne closed her eyes and clung to the saddle horn as the horse lurched forward. Okay, maybe it wasn't lurching. Maybe she should look.

But that meant she was staring straight at the back of the cowboy who held her son in his hopefully secure grasp.

WELL, wasn't this quite the turn of events? Never in a million years would Blake have guessed Nathaniel's fiancée would befriend the woman who'd publicly dumped him on the floor, never mind bring her to Rockstead Ranch and put her at Blake's mercy.

Oh, the things he could do to make Emma's mare, Desiree, side-step or break into a trot. Not that he would, of course. He wasn't mean. But it was a tiny bit tempting to even the score and see how *she'd* feel toppled to the ground, staring up at him instead of the other way around.

But, no. He wouldn't. After all, she'd just been reacting to his ill-conceived attention when he'd thought she was Marnie. He could see it must have been a shock to find a stranger's arms around her middle while he kissed her neck.

Her waist was mighty trim with that gray T-shirt tucked into those jeans. He hadn't quite wrapped his hands around it when he lifted her, but it had been close. He'd inhaled a whiff of lilac before her fingers skewered his shoulders and her nearness drove away all conscious thought.

Nah. He wasn't reacting to her. Not that way. He didn't date prissy girls. He definitely didn't date single moms, and her son sat wedged in front of Blake in the saddle this very minute.

In fact, the kid was chattering a hundred miles an hour, and he'd probably been doing that for the past five minutes. Blake tried to tune in.

"...is so cool! What's your horse's name?"

"Zorro." Blake glanced behind him.

Dafne clung to the saddle horn with both hands, her eyes closed, her face pale and tight.

He could almost feel sorry for her.

"That's a nice name. Is it a boy or a girl?"

"Boy." Blake wasn't going to explain the difference between stallions and geldings to the child.

"How old is Zorro?"

Blake blinked. Did this boy never stop asking questions? He made Toby seem deaf and mute, which was far from the case. "He's eight. Now, look around at the trees and the sky. If you're really quiet, we might see a deer or an eagle."

"Okay!"

Speaking of deer, it was nearly hunting season. Dad had a weakness for wild meat, sort of like old Isaac in the Bible. About the only way Blake got extra time off of work was for hunting. He could hardly wait to ride out to the trappers cabin in the high ranges, just him and Zorro for a few days. He'd kind of made it a habit not to shoot the first buck he saw, because that meant he needed to pack the animal down to the ranch. Which meant his hunting and camping was over for the season.

He glanced at Dafne again. This time her eyes were squinted, like she was trying to get up the nerve to look around her. "How's it going?" he asked casually.

"Okay."

Blake managed not to laugh at the sight of her frozen face. Did she think even moving her eyes or mouth might be enough to cause her to lose her balance? "You can relax. Desiree's good. She won't let you fall."

Behind Dafne came Toby on Clover, then Ainsley and Bella on Domino. They all looked like they were doing fine. He refocused on Dafne. "Look around you. Hear the meadowlarks. Feel the breeze rippling through the aspens. Smell the mountain air. I bet you don't get that in Spokane."

Her eyes flew open. "How do you know where I'm from?"

Caught, but he didn't much care. "The twins talked about you last weekend when they were home."

Dafne almost smiled. "They hate me."

"Oh, I wouldn't go that far. They've just got a lot to adjust to right now." Then Dafne would probably be their favorite teacher. How could she not be? If she brought out her fire and passion in class, she'd make all the kids fall in love with her. Her fire and passion were conspicuously missing at the moment, but Blake had no doubt they lingered just below the surface, ready to erupt at any moment like Mount St Helens. He grinned.

"What's so funny?"

Observant minx. "Just waiting for you to relax a little."

"I'm relaxed."

Now he chuckled out loud. "All evidence to the contrary?"

"How do you get used to this?"

Blake shifted a little so he could see her better without kinking his neck. "I've been riding since I was younger than Bella. By myself since I was about three. I used to climb on the fence or an overturned bucket to get on Rocky's back. Whatever I could find."

"Did you ever fall off?"

"Only about a hundred times, probably. But not lately."

The little boy in front of him tipped his head back to look into Blake's eyes. "Did Toby ever fall off?"

"Sure. Everything you try to do that's hard, you run the risk of falling. Otherwise, you never learn anything new."

"I don't want to fall."

"Falling hurts." Blake couldn't resist the dig. "The other day I fell on a cement floor. Boy, did my tailbone ever hurt." Also, his pride.

"You did?" The boy's eyes widened.

"Yeah. I limped for two days."

"About that…" Dafne said from behind him.

Aha, she *had* been listening still.

"I didn't mean to."

"Sure, you didn't."

"I mean, imagine being new to town, everything is strange, and you're minding your own business and texting with your sister, when all of a sudden someone grabs you from behind and… nuzzles you?"

Blake smirked. "Shocking, for sure. I doubt it will ever happen again. The nuzzler" — wasn't that a great word? — "isn't likely to make the same mistake twice."

Next time, he was going to kiss her like he meant it.

Hold on a second, cowboy. Next time? With Dafne? Nuh uh. She was totally not his kind of woman. He had that whole list, remember? But flitting from one to the next like some kind of bumblebee in a patch of wildflowers wasn't satisfying anymore.

The kind of woman who only wanted a good time was obviously not the sort of woman who was into commitment. What was the saying? A guy couldn't keep doing the same thing over and over and expect different results.

But who said he wanted different results? Desired commitment?

The little boy wedged in front of him glanced up with eager, trusting eyes and a wide grin.

The woman on the mare behind him was less trusting, probably with a whole bunch of good reasons.

But Blake could be worth trusting, couldn't he?

CHAPTER SEVEN

"I miss riding." Kathryn tucked her feet up under herself on Ainsley's sofa.

The three teen girls were upstairs in Vivienne's room, and Ainsley had just tucked Bella in bed.

Gavin glanced up from playing a game on Dafne's iPad. "I like horses," he announced.

Dafne sighed. Of course, he did. Hadn't horses been practically at the top of her *never* list? And not only had she survived an hour in the saddle herself, but her son had spent the same hour held in the casual, but secure, grip of the cowboy Dafne had decked when she first came to town.

And he'd had the nerve to tease her about it. She'd been clinging to the experience to demonstrate all that was wrong with Jewel Lake — even though it had fully been her choice to move here — and now she'd been forced to realize the evil perp was just an average guy who'd mistaken her identity. Or maybe not-so-average, since Gavin had decided Mr. Blake was right up there with God, having hung the sun, moon, and stars. How else would Gavin have seen, not only a still-spotted fawn and a chattery gray squirrel, but a bald eagle looking down at them from the top of a tall, dead tree before it took to flight, swooping majestically beside them?

"Dafne did a great job for her first ride." Ainsley set a plate of muffins on the coffee table. "Next time, she'll feel even more secure."

"There won't be a next time." The answer was automatic.

"But, Mama!" Gavin's eyes filled with tears as he looked up at her. "Can I go without you?"

"Um." All eyes in the room were upon her. "We'll see."

"You can't be a Montana girl without riding once in a while." Ainsley's eyebrows peaked.

"No one gave me the rulebook in advance." Dafne managed a chuckle.

"I promised the twins I'd take them up this weekend for a ride," Kathryn went on. "I miss the ranch as much as they do."

Surely the older woman didn't miss that surly husband she'd left. The ranch, maybe, but even that was hard to imagine. The scenery was beyond comparison, though, and Blake said just wait until frost turned the larch golden. Probably Dafne could enjoy the view from her own windows, which looked toward the lake and a tree-covered mountain beyond it.

"In fact, I was thinking more about the high-school retreat." Kathryn peeled back the paper liner from around a muffin. "There's a trappers cabin way back on the ranch with an amazing view of Glacier National Park. I think it would be a great base for that weekend."

Dafne opened her mouth and closed it again. What amenities, exactly, did a trappers cabin have? Probably not electricity or indoor plumbing. She'd read the Little House on the Prairie books when she was a kid. They'd helped ignite her passion for history while making her extremely thankful to be an urban child of the twenty-first century.

"I'll ask the boys and see if one of them would help with hauling in supplies and help overseeing it. I doubt we can talk Mr. Winslow into coming along."

The science teacher must be five minutes from retiring. He walked slightly stooped over... Dafne couldn't imagine him hiking around on uneven trails back in the mountains.

She couldn't imagine herself doing that, and she was young and fit. There wouldn't be horses involved, would there? She eyed Kathryn.

"Blake probably would," Ainsley said casually. "He seems at loose ends these days."

Dafne sharpened her gaze on Ainsley, who kept looking at Kathryn.

"I was thinking of Ryder," Kathryn replied.

"He doesn't have near the experience in the mountains. I bet Blake would do a great job."

"You think?" Kathryn looked between Ainsley and Dafne.

"Absolutely. But you can broach the subject yourself. He's in town with Nathaniel, and they're stopping by shortly."

News to Dafne. Was Ainsley matchmaking? Some people couldn't help themselves. Well, Dafne would straighten Ainsley out later, because no one was going to meddle in Dafne's love life and get away with it. Even though she'd told Ainsley she was absolutely not interested in dating, it seemed her new friend didn't quite believe her.

"I like Mr. Blake." Gavin looked up from the iPad. "He knows lotsa stuff about the woods."

"He sure does." Ainsley sounded a little too enthusiastic for someone engaged to the man's brother. If he was so great, why wasn't Ainsley marrying Blake instead?

There was a quiet tap at the door before it opened, and Nathaniel stepped inside. Dafne had met Ainsley's fiancé a couple of times now. When the man's gaze went straight for Ainsley, latched on, and was exchanged in intensity, Dafne knew there was no way her friend had a thing for Blake. Which meant her words were definitely intended for Dafne.

The cowboy in question came in behind his brother, and this man's eyes focused instantaneously on Dafne. She raised her eyebrows in challenge and met his gaze. He wasn't going to intimidate her or seduce her. There was no way on earth she was going to be another checkmark on the guy's list of conquests. He had a reputation she wanted nothing to do with.

"Mr. Blake!" Gavin thrust the tablet aside and charged at the cowboy.

"Hey, squirt." Blake scooped the six-year-old up as though he weighed no more than a kitten and set Gavin on his shoulders.

Gavin lifted Blake's cowboy hat and set it on his own head, and the man squinted up at him. "Hey, you stole my hat."

The boy giggled. "It was in my way. Do I look like a cowboy now?"

Blake seemed to consider his reply as he studied Gavin. "You know, you kind of do. What do you think, Dafne?"

She did not want to get involved in this little game. She'd meant to keep her precious son far away from ranches, horses, and especially cowboys. *Way to fail, Daf.*

Was it her job to coddle her boy? Probably not, but this wasn't the way she'd have chosen to expand Gavin's horizons. Not with a handsome cowboy who spelled nothing but trouble for her son's mama.

The reasons for that were not something she wished to examine. Not with Ainsley and Nathaniel in the room. And not with Kathryn, who watched the scenario with something like understanding passing over her face.

Great someone understood what was going on, because Dafne definitely did not. And mostly, she didn't want to.

THE KID CHATTERED on and on in Blake's ear, firing questions as though from a sub-machine gun. No way Blake could have answered a single one before ten more took its place.

"Gavin. Let the poor man think."

Poor man, huh? Blake grinned at Dafne. Then he caught his stepmom's curious expression. Uh. It would never do to have Kathryn speculating on Blake's interest in the pretty newcomer. If only he could keep thinking of Dafne that way, it would help. Prissy city girl. Stuck-up. Violent.

No matter how he clung to that image, it drifted away

like the wisps of fog in a mountain meadow on a frosty autumn morning. And just like the mist being nudged away by the rising sun glistening on the frosty grasses, the fog in his head dissipated and revealed a pretty, feisty, woman.

With a kid.

Blake hoisted Gavin off of his shoulders. Before he could retrieve his hat, the boy darted away, giggling, clamping it on his head. He could chase him down and rescue it, but what did it hurt? He'd only have to hang it on the rack by the door anyway.

Why had he let Nathaniel talk him into swinging by Ainsley's place? Had he been hoping to see Dafne? He hadn't let himself think about his reasons up at the ranch. He was bored, that was all. He needed a girlfriend or two.

"Question for you, Blake." Kathryn patted the sofa beside her.

That would put him between his stepmother and the teacher. Not happening, not when there was a vacant easy chair across the room. He settled into it, ignoring the sight of Nathaniel and Ainsley smooching on the love seat. He didn't want to look at Dafne, either. Imagine a group where the person he most wanted to focus on was his stepmother? He'd never have guessed that could happen.

"Priscilla Cantrell asked Dafne and me to create a weekend getaway for the high-school students. We were thinking a weekend up at the trappers cabin might be fun."

Dafne made a little snort as she shifted in her seat, not looking at him.

Blake suppressed a grin. Kathryn's idea, not Dafne's.

Check. "Oh, yeah? How many kids? When are you thinking?"

"There are 47 teens in the high school division. I doubt they'd all come, but we should plan on 50 including chaperones."

"The cabin's not that big."

"I know." Kathryn shook her head. "But it does have a wood stove and a table and a bit of counter space for meal prep. Having walls should keep the food away from bears. The kids can bring tents."

Dafne jumped to her feet. "Bears? You're not worried about keeping *people* away from bears? Just food?"

Blake smirked. She was starting to clue in where she was going to sleep. "Kids aren't quite as tasty, especially with tents and sleeping bags to get caught in the grizzly's teeth."

Her eyes widened, and her mouth dropped open as she stared at him.

"Blake," Kathryn chided. "Don't terrify the poor girl."

"You can count me out." Dafne backed up a step. "This isn't my thing. At all."

Blake stretched out his legs and crossed them at the ankles as he folded his hands behind his head. "Bears usually avoid people. They're really only looking for an easy handout most of the time. So, if food is stored out of reach, they'll meander on."

Her eyebrows hiked. "Usually."

"That's what I said. There's an occasional rogue, but it's not likely that far back in the mountains, since they haven't experienced sloppy campers for the most part. Besides..." He studied her. Could she take a joke? If not, he needed to find out now. "Besides, you're a jiu jitsu master. You could take down an unsuspecting grizz in two seconds flat."

Her narrowed eyes glittered dangerously.

So… maybe she couldn't laugh at herself. Maybe she took *everything* seriously, not just guys who startled her.

"Jiu jitsu?" Now was a fine time for Ainsley to enter the conversation. "I've always wanted to learn one of those martial arts."

"You should," Blake drawled, gaze fixed on Dafne. "It's pretty effective on a brute six inches taller and fifty pounds heavier. Right, Dafne?"

Her cheeks flushed to scarlet in an instant.

Nathaniel burst out laughing. "Oh, no way. *You're* the woman. Noah saw the whole thing."

"And couldn't wait to tell you and everyone else, I imagine." Whatever embarrassment Blake had suffered was long gone. Now it was just a great story to tell.

Dafne darted a glance at Kathryn. "I'm not sure this is a good idea. I've never been camping, and I don't think I want to start now. Besides, I can't take Gavin, and I have nowhere to leave him."

"I bet he'd love to stay with Toby." Ainsley glanced between them. "Ask Dakota. All she can say is yes or no."

"I don't really know them that well."

"Or he can stay with Bella and me. It would be fun to have him."

Blake tried to keep his mouth shut. Really, he did. But it just wasn't in his nature. He leaned forward, elbows on his knees. "If you've never been camping, this would be the perfect time to give it a try. Pretty sure we could rustle up a tent and bedroll for you, so that's no excuse. Besides, there's nothing more beautiful than being in the high country with the leaves just starting to turn and the early morning mist lifting off the valleys. It's my favorite place and my favorite time of year."

"Sounds like you're volunteering to help with the retreat?" his stepmother asked.

His gaze latched onto Dafne's again. "Sure, why not? I can haul supplies up with the quad and trailer. Make sure there's firewood for cooking and bonfires. Stuff like that."

"It's not too far to hike in, is it?"

He glanced at Kathryn. "Not really. Two, three hours, tops. The teens probably all have backpacks. They can carry most of their own stuff. Or toss it in the trailer."

Kathryn nodded. "What do you say, Dafne? Are you in, or do I need to ask Mr. Winslow?"

"Winslow?" Blake couldn't keep the incredulity from his voice. "You're kidding, right? There's no way he could walk five minutes, let alone the five hours it would take him to get to the cabin. Aren't there any other teachers you could ask? Isn't Eli teaching some of the Bible classes?"

Way to open his big mouth. Eli Bryson was Creekside Fellowship's youth pastor. Young. Vibrant. No way should Blake bring the guy to Dafne's attention or vice versa.

And... why was that? Eli made no secret he was keeping an eye out for the right woman. He'd be perfect for Dafne and Gavin. A model Christian.

But something in Blake made him wonder if there was any chance the teacher might see something worthwhile in him, not Eli.

He wasn't actually thinking of settling down himself, was he? Nah. It was just that he wasn't used to women rejecting him, and that had happened a little too often lately. So, it was the thrill of the chase. What would happen if he actually caught her?

He'd kiss her. And maybe he'd be a goner.

Probably not.

But maybe.

CHAPTER EIGHT

Dafne should move back to the city, where no one had ever once tried to convince her to go horseback riding, let alone two weekends in a row. Around here, people assumed she'd be eager or at least willing.

She should be glad that Blake was nowhere to be seen when she, Kathryn, the twins, and Gavin pulled into the ranch yard and parked by the corral. The girls piled out of the SUV and charged for the stable.

"Those kids." Kathryn shook her head as she beckoned Gavin out of the middle before shutting both doors on her side.

Dafne took a deep breath and looked around. Not for Blake, of course. But he'd been such a distraction last time that she hadn't really contemplated her surroundings. Across the parking area sat a very large house nestled beneath even taller trees. Kathryn had given that up for the two-bedroom apartment she shared with the girls in town?

She must have been desperate to get away from the twins' father.

The road continued on around a curve beside the trees, which was where they'd ridden last week — past a row of small log cabins, a huge barn, and an equally large shed filled with equipment. Then the road had narrowed, crossed a creek, and started to wind up the hill. Maybe they were going that way again.

She focused on the stable and corral to the left, where the twins were already leading out the two horses she and Ainsley had ridden last week.

Dafne swallowed a dose of panic. How had she blocked out she'd be riding something different this time? Everyone assumed she could do this, but she wasn't so sure. Still, she couldn't back out now. Not with Gavin clinging to the corral rails like a monkey as the girls hugged their horses' necks.

Kathryn had disappeared into the stable, so Dafne came up beside Gavin.

He beamed up at her. "Hi, Mama! Those horses are so cool. Can I ride Toby's pony? He wouldn't mind, right? He's not here."

"Oh, no, definitely not. It takes a long time to learn how to ride a pony by yourself." Decades, if she could help it.

"But Toby's only five, and I'm six."

"That's true, but—"

"And *you* rode all by yourself last time."

"I'm a grownup." She didn't feel like it at times, but whatever. It was still true.

Emma glanced over. "I could saddle up Clover for him."

"Thanks, but no. He's going to ride with your mom. She offered."

"All right." The teen adjusted her mare's stirrups and swung up. "Ready, Lex?"

"Yup." Alexia leaned into the open stable door. "See you up there, Mom." Alexia mounted up, and the two girls trotted away.

"That's so cool," breathed Gavin, eyes wide.

Kathryn came out of the stable leading two horses, both already saddled. "Need a hand up?"

"I… um…" Could Dafne do this on her own? The others made it look so easy. "I can try."

Kathryn nodded and extended a pair of reins toward Dafne. "Here you go."

"Wait, no. I don't know what to do."

"Put your left foot in the stirrup. Grab the saddle horn. Swing your right leg over the top."

She couldn't. She didn't want to. Her child was watching. She could. She had to. She *must*.

Dafne took a deep breath and offered a terse nod before sticking her shoe in the leather stirrup. She grabbed the saddle horn and, with a prayer and a ton of effort, she somehow got herself up on top of the horse. It wasn't graceful, but she succeeded.

She let out the air she'd been holding and accepted the reins Kathryn offered her. Now she'd be in charge of its speed and direction, too? She swallowed the panic.

"You'll be fine, Dafne. Lady is one of our oldest horses. She's just going to plod along behind Laire. I promise."

"Okay."

"You did it, Mama! All by yourself."

She *had*. Dafne straightened her back and grinned down at Gavin. "Thanks, baby."

Kathryn lifted Gavin to her saddle and easily mounted behind him. She smiled at Dafne, clicked her tongue, and set off.

Lady stood with her head down. This didn't look anything like following.

"Just give her a very gentle nudge with your heels."

Wouldn't that spook the old horse? But nothing was happening the way it was. Dafne tapped her heels, imagining herself Dorothy in sparkly ruby shoes, wishing to return to Kansas. Only, in Dafne's case, that would be Spokane.

Lady lumbered into motion.

"Good job, Mama!"

Kathryn's smile meant almost as much as Gavin's encouragement. Now all Dafne had to do was stay seated. She could do this.

UGH. Too hot. Too sweaty. Blake yanked his T-shirt over his head and tossed it in the shade near where Zorro cropped the meadow grass.

Ryder ran the chainsaw, cutting downed trees into lengths that would fit in the cabin's old cookstove.

Blake trimmed the branch stubs off of one length, then set it on the chopping block. With a sharp swing of his axe, the log split in two. He grabbed one of the halves and repeated the process. The wood needed to be fairly small to fit in the stove's firebox and maintain even heat.

He settled into a rhythm, tossing the chopped firewood into a pile off to one side, lulled by the zing of the chainsaw. They didn't need a ton for a weekend getaway, but he'd made it a habit to refresh the woodpile up here every fall. A guy never knew when he'd be stranded by a winter storm while working the cows and need the nearest shelter. After the teens were done with the place, he'd stock it with some sealed containers of jerky, dried fruit, and hardtack. Those needed to be kept out of reach of rodents and bears alike.

Ryder set the saw down, the silence deafening. "You've got the right idea." He peeled off his own T-shirt then tugged his leather gloves back on. "Sure hot for the middle of September. It's hard to remember how cold it can get up here."

Blake grunted and split another log. He'd spent a few sub-zero nights at the cabin on more than one occasion. The winter cold was real.

His brother began stacking the chopped wood. "You haven't been dating lately."

"Your business how?"

Ryder laughed. "Just an observation."

Blake shrugged. Split another log.

"What did you think of Pastor Smith's sermon on Sunday?"

Did he look like someone who wanted to chitchat about the Bible — or anything else — today? He doubted it. But the sermon on Colossians 3 had caught his attention more than many had recently. "Doing everything in God's name?"

"Yeah. Not just doing good stuff, but doing it well, for God."

Blake certainly hadn't been dating well, which was likely why the sermon had stuck in his brain like a burr in a horse's mane. Maybe he hadn't been doing much of anything well, just putting in time. Drifting along.

Sure, the ranch work was getting done. They'd gotten the hay off of the fields, the fences repaired, and the new windmill installed for extracting well water for the cattle and horses even when the power went out, which was fairly frequent in the winter. Because Rockstead was so far off the highway, they weren't top priority for the power company. Dad had been building up the ranch's self-sufficiency over the past few years, more for the stock's comfort than the family's.

That was Dad's way. He'd probably be living in a bunkhouse himself if Mom hadn't pushed for the mansion before they married. Now he rattled around in that huge house all by himself, since his sons had moved into the row of cabins by the creek and his daughters lived in town.

Did Blake really want to end up bitter and alone like Dad? Not so much. What were the options? Blake had tried the ever-young approach with all his casual dating the past few years. He was kind of over all that already. Which meant he had the choice of swearing off women forever, or going all in with just one.

Why did the pretty teacher pop into his mind with that thought? She wasn't what he was looking for. Except, why not? He'd never dated a single mom, but that only made sense with his no-entanglements policy. If he were going all in, then he wasn't going to crush some kid's heart.

Blake kept swinging the axe, kept tossing split logs toward his brother, who kept building the stack.

Had Dad ever gone all in? He probably thought he had, at least with Mom. Then why hadn't it worked? Probably because Dad was first married to the ranch and figured everything else should get in line, including his wife. And because Dad was selfish. Mom had been, too. She'd come around once last year, and wowza. There'd been a lot of yelling and cursing from both of them. Shadows of Blake's childhood.

He glugged a quart of water from his canteen and went back to work, thankful his kid brother had shut up and was focused on his task.

Blake wasn't as selfish as his parents, was he?

Ouch. He didn't want to think about that. He might try to defend his lifestyle by saying he didn't want the girls he dated to be hurt, but whom had he really been trying to protect? Blake Daniel Cavanagh. And if that wasn't arrogance, what was?

And whatever you do, whether in word or deed, do it all in the name of the Lord Jesus, giving thanks to God the Father through him.

Okay, fine, he'd been selfish by dabbling and playing around. He certainly hadn't been dating in the name of the Lord Jesus. Did he want to change? It had to be better than the alternatives.

Change was hard. He didn't really want to.

It had been hard for his brothers. For Adam, for Travis, and for Nathaniel. But they all agreed that it was worth it. They were happier now, and not just because of the love of a good woman, but because they were focused on following God.

Again, his mind swung to Dafne Santoro. She'd been in church the past couple of Sundays, leaning forward with her Bible open on her lap as she took in Pastor Marshall's words. Evidence said she was focused on following God, too.

What about Blake?

He heard the horses approaching before he saw his twin sisters emerging into the clearing on Domino and Desiree. They'd be smart enough to stay clear of flying firewood. He nodded in their direction and took a crack at the next log.

The girls walked their mares into the creek and let them drink their fill before guiding them back to the shade and dismounting near Zorro and Champlain.

Alexia dropped to the cabin steps. "Mom and Ms. Santoro will be here in a few minutes."

Blake grunted an acknowledgment, ignoring Ryder's quick smirk in his direction. His kid brother didn't know anything. No one did, least of all Blake.

But, hey, he had to give Dafne chops for getting on a horse again. She'd been totally terrified last week. His estimation of her ticked up a notch. The woman had grit and determination. Or maybe she just didn't want to look bad in front of her kid.

Gavin was a cute little monkey and plenty daring to steal a cowboy's hat. Of course, Spokane probably wasn't big on cowboys, so maybe he just didn't know better... but weren't guys everywhere possessive of whatever hats they wore, even baseball caps?

How many men had been in the little tyke's life? No dad in sight, but that didn't mean there hadn't been one recently.

Blake was crazy to be thinking this way. He was the independent one, remember? No woman was going to tie him down and tame him. He might not share Dad's personality like Travis did, but he still had some of his sire's traits. An ego the size of Montana might be one of those.

He heard the voices and hoofbeats before the other two horses entered the clearing. Kathryn came first, sitting tall with little Gavin in front of her, the kid beaming from ear to ear. And then Dafne on Lady, looking as terrified and rigid as she had last week.

Blake whacked the axe deep into the chopping block and strode over, stretching his hands for the boy.

"Hi, Mr. Blake! I rided on Laire! And I didn't even fall off."

"Good job, squirt." Blake turned toward Dafne.

"You're all sweaty, Mr. Blake."

Dafne's eyes widened as she took him in. Or was the look for her son? Uh... right. Blake had nearly forgotten he'd stripped his shirt off an hour ago. Well, if she wanted to stare at his bare chest, he wouldn't stop her.

Blake leaned to lower the boy to the ground. "Careful of the logs, and don't touch the axe."

"Okay!" Gavin darted to where Emma and Alexia slouched on the steps.

"Need a hand down?" Blake asked Dafne. Was she flushed from the heat or from looking at him? This could be fun. He grinned and hooked his finger through Lady's bridle. "Your call." Either way, he was gonna stay smack in her line of vision.

Her gaze flicked to his face then away toward the creek. "Help, please."

"My pleasure." And he meant that in the sincerest way possible. And if she brushed a little close to him as he lifted her from the saddle, that wasn't a problem. At least not for him.

She stumbled a little as he set her on the ground, which meant he had to keep on steadying her. A gentleman wouldn't let her fall as she tried to regain her land-legs.

If they didn't have an audience, he'd have been tempted to kiss her. Okay, he was tempted, anyway, but good sense prevailed. This wasn't the moment. Not with Kathryn and Ryder and the twins and the kid all watching.

It was still hard to let go of her trim waist. "You good now?"

She glanced at him and pushed his hands away with her own. "Fine. Thank you."

"Any time." He tore his gaze away from her blue eyes and took in the others.

The twins dug their elbows into each other's sides and giggled as they watched him.

Blake was in for it now.

CHAPTER NINE

That darn cowboy had gone shirtless on purpose. He had to have, by the smirk on his face as he let her go. It hadn't escaped Dafne's notice that his rippling pecs and biceps were bronzed and glistening in the sun.

Not that she was going to sneak another glimpse. Not if she had to count every log in the woodpile to avoid seeing him.

She'd met Ryder briefly the other day. At least the younger cowboy had the good grace to tug a sweat-stained T-shirt over his head now. Unlike his brother.

Hitching her shoulder to block her view, she handed Lady's reins to Kathryn and crossed to the little cabin. This was going to be headquarters for fifty people for an entire weekend? Not a chance. The whole thing looked smaller than Mom's living room back home and, while they occasionally packed the entire Santoro clan in there for a couple of hours, it didn't leave much available air.

Dafne was already struggling for oxygen. She'd like to

chalk it up to altitude, but it was likely the cocky cowboy she was trying to avoid looking at. If this was how she got the minute she was away from home and on her own, no wonder her parents had been against her taking this job so far from Spokane. She obviously couldn't be trusted.

"Look at all the pretty leaves, Mama!"

Gavin. Yes. She smiled at her young son as he jumped up to meet her. "It is very pretty." The aspens around the cabin were already golden, gleaming in the September sunshine. The leaves trembled in the barest of breezes. Although today was plenty warm, as evidenced by the bare-chested man she was *not* looking at, there were plenty of hints that cooler days were on their way.

It was, quite simply, invigorating.

Kathryn opened the door to the cabin and stepped inside. Dafne turned the long way around to avoid the guys and followed the older woman inside.

"Girls!" called Kathryn. "Can you open the shutters, please?"

"Sure," replied one of the twins. A minute later light came in from behind the small table, then more from another window.

Kathryn planted her hands on her hips and surveyed the space. "What do you think?"

Dafne was pretty sure the woman didn't really want to know. "Um, it needs cleaning?"

"It does, at that." Kathryn chuckled. "Emma, grab a few sticks of wood and let's get a fire going."

A fire? It wasn't that cold.

"To heat water for scrubbing."

Of course. Dafne tried to channel her inner Laura Ingalls. "With creek water?"

"There's a gravity-fed tank just up the hillside. The boys drain it over the winter or the pipes freeze and break, but it's a good system for the warmer months."

Dafne nodded as though she understood. But some semblance of running water sounded good, even though it didn't likely translate into steaming showers or flush toilets.

The girls entered, each carrying an armload of wood. Gavin looked eagerly around.

Her boy was soaking up this wilderness experience. Dafne would chalk it up to being a Y-chromosome thing if Kathryn weren't in the process of opening a little door on the old-fashioned cookstove and putting in a few thin sticks of wood. She tucked in a piece of crumpled newspaper and lit a match to it. Hungry flames engulfed the paper and began to catch on the wood.

"There." Kathryn sounded satisfied. "When we're here for the entire weekend, we'll fill this reservoir with water so it heats up whenever we're cooking, but for today, we'll just use the kettle." She ran water from the faucet until it cleared then filled a blackened kettle and set it on the stove. "That will take a bit of time, so let's look around. Did you see there's a loft?"

Dafne looked up. Sure enough, half the space had a lower ceiling with a ladder leading up to it.

"Can I see what's up there, Mama?" Gavin tugged on her hand.

"I'll show him," Emma said.

Dafne followed them up just far enough to see there

was no railing and only a couple of bed-sized platforms with no mattresses on them. "Be careful."

"I will, Mama."

Of course, he would. He was buzzing with all the new experiences in his life, but he was basically a cautious child. Probably from having a mother who hovered over him. Well, she'd moved to Montana, right? If that wasn't giving both of them more freedom than before, she didn't know what was.

A shadow darkened the doorway, and she glanced over as her feet landed back on the weathered plank floor.

Blake. At least he'd put his T-shirt back on. He grinned at her as though he were perfectly aware of her thought process. Then he focused on his stepmother. "Need anything else, Kathryn?"

"Are you tall enough to sweep the cobwebs off the middle of the ceiling?

"Sure. Nice change from chopping wood."

"I appreciate that woodpile out there. It's way more than we'll need for a weekend."

He shrugged, again glancing at Dafne. "We make sure to replenish it every fall, regardless. Just did a little extra."

Dafne frowned. "Does someone live here in the winter?" Surely not.

Blake shook his head. "No, but we ride out this way from time to time, and you never know when the weather might catch a cowboy out this far. That's why we keep the cabin up."

"And Blakey likes to stay here when he goes hunting." Alexia crossed her arms and raised her eyebrows at her brother. "He pretends he's all macho, sleeping under the stars and all that, but pretty sure he's a softie underneath it all."

"Don't you remember camping with Nathaniel and me in July? It wasn't that long ago. There wasn't a cabin in sight." He lifted a broom off a hook behind the door and gently whacked Alexia with it.

She winced away. "We also weren't out this direction." She paused. "I don't think."

He snorted a laugh and looked up to the roof's peak. "You all might want to stay clear of whatever might come down."

His interaction with his sisters reminded her of how Peter was with her when she was little. Her big brother had turned out to be an awesome, responsible adult, even though he'd given up a government job with Fish and Wildlife to start his own business with two of their cousins. And he'd been married to an attorney for almost four years now.

What would Peter think of Blake?

Dafne blinked.

Not that it mattered. It wasn't like she was interested in the cocky cowboy. Just because she was staring at him.

Blake flashed her a grin, and she looked away. He was only eye-candy, right? And Dafne wasn't interested. First, she needed to prove to her parents and to herself that she could take care of herself and Gavin. There'd be time for falling in love later.

Much later.

RYDER and the twins rode further up the mountain trail, taking the long loop back. Blake should have gone with them or headed down to the ranch once the cabin was freshened, but no. It seemed like Dafne exuded some kind of magnetic force over him, causing him to linger in her presence.

Her kid was entertaining, too. A little older than Toby and a little wiser in some ways, Gavin had a pure innocence about the trees, the mountains, the horses — about all of nature. He took everything in with a sense of delighted wonder that was kind of fun to feed.

Blake showed Gavin and his mom the water tank and how it was filled from the stream above a tumbling set of falls. He explained about the outhouse tucked across the clearing — that was going to be tricky with fifty people around the cabin. He should dig another pit and hang a tarp around it so there could at least be a girls' room and a boys' room. He added the task to his mental to-do list.

The boy was enthralled with the privy, his mother less so. Blake laughed. She was such a city girl... but she was game; he'd give her that much. She was terrified of the horses, had ducked away from the stray spiders he'd dislodged from the cabin's rafters, and darted nervous glances into the trees whenever he mentioned bears. But she was still here.

That she also sidled a little closer to him only made him mention bears a couple of more times. Hey, you couldn't blame a guy for trying.

Kathryn came out of the cabin and bolted the door behind her. They never locked it — that ran against both the trappers code and the cowboy code. Shelter could mean life or death if someone was stranded in the high mountains, whether it was a lost hiker or whomever.

She looked around with satisfaction. "There. I think I'll be able to stand coming in there now with the teens, but we'll need to be super organized with all the food and supplies."

Dafne darted a glance between Blake and Kathryn. "Who's sleeping up in that loft? Any chance I—"

"I think we'll need to stay in the tents with the girls. Otherwise, they might get up to shenanigans in the middle of the night." Kathryn paused, frowning. "We are definitely going to need a couple of men along to chaperone the boys."

Blake knew how Charlie Bucket felt when he found the golden ticket to tour the chocolate factory. "Yeah, you probably do. I could probably wrangle a day or two from Dad and give you a hand. Maybe Ryder or Noah could come, too."

"Oh, would you? That would be a huge relief. I know there are some male teachers, but I don't know any of them well enough to ask, and I don't want anyone thinking anything... improper."

Because his stepmother was loyal to his father, even when the man didn't deserve it. She said she'd said her vows and meant them, that a person didn't throw out the baby with the bathwater when times got tough.

Which meant she'd moved into town with the girls without filing for divorce. That was going to have to come from Dad, apparently. It was going to be interesting watching this play out, but one thing Blake knew — Kathryn was a whole lot stronger than he'd been thinking for the past few years. She'd finally had enough of Dad's surly ways, grown a backbone, and moved out. Frankly, that backbone looked good on her. Who'd have thought?

Blake scanned the clearing. The windows were shuttered, the firewood stacked, and the pipes to the water tank diverted. "Ready to head back to the ranch?"

Kathryn nodded. "You want to hand Gavin up to me?"

"Nah, I'll take him." Blake picked the boy up and swung him to one shoulder.

Gavin chortled with glee and grabbed Blake's hat.

Blake couldn't find it in himself to get after the kid for it. He set him onto Zorro's saddle. "Sit tight, and I'll give your mom a hand."

Dafne took a deep breath. "I can do this myself."

"Okay." Blake shifted closer.

"Really, I can. I did at the ranch."

"Good for you. I'll be here in case."

"I don't need help."

He managed not to grin. "I believe you. Go for it."

She shot him a look, biting her lip. Then she grabbed the saddle horn, stuck her foot in the stirrup, and tried to heave herself up.

Was she going to make it? She seemed stuck.

Blake's hands clenched and unclenched. Should he? How could he not?

Dafne struggled to get enough momentum to swing her leg over the saddle.

Finally, he couldn't resist any longer. "Here." He lifted her the rest of the way.

"I didn't need help." Her face fiery, she stared past his head as she gathered the reins.

"I know." Yeah, he was lying.

"But, thank you."

"You're welcome." Blake resisted the impulse to leap onto Zorro without using the stirrups, but he hadn't done that in years, and he definitely didn't want to jump and land wrong.

Not in front of Dafne.

So, he swung into the saddle like a normal human being and nestled the little boy against his chest as he gathered the reins. "Ready?" He glanced at Dafne then at Kathryn.

His stepmother raised her eyebrows at him and glanced between him and Dafne.

Ah, she thought she knew something?

Blake raised his eyebrows back at her and kept his expressions as bland as possible.

So, his crush on the teacher was showing. Sue him.

CHAPTER TEN

Dafne sat rigid in the saddle, even if that meant she was fighting Lady's gait. Behind her, Gavin chattered at Blake, asking a thousand questions about the trees and the birds and the creek they rode beside.

Her ears tuned to Blake's deeper voice responding patiently — not to every question, as that would have been impossible. Gavin fired them without waiting for a reply. Still, whenever Gavin paused for breath, Blake answered or pointed out something her son hadn't even noticed yet.

That she hadn't noticed, either, because she was so focused on the cowboy behind her. How could the man be so patient with Gavin? Even Dad and Peter didn't last this long before ruffling Gavin's hair and telling him it was enough for now.

Blake would reach the end of his patience long before the end of the trail. Right?

Ahead, Kathryn turned Laire off the trail into a small clearing by the creek.

Lady plodded in behind the leader, and Dafne breathed a sigh of relief when Kathryn dismounted and stretched. She could use the break, too, except it meant one more time off and on the horse. Still, she couldn't very well stay on Lady's back while the others dismounted.

Before she'd managed to remember which leg to swing over the horse's back, Blake stood beside her and reached up for her.

Don't think too much about it, Dafne. She allowed him to help her off. This time, he didn't linger but turned back to catch Gavin, who launched into his arms.

She didn't want to watch this cowboy woo her son. This was the guy who Dafne had flattened in the coffee shop. Whose girlfriend had broken up with him in public. She'd heard a rumor or two — not that she was seeking them out, of course — that Blake had a reputation with the ladies.

This was not the kind of man she should let Gavin get attached to, never mind herself. She was only twenty-three. She needed to live and work in Jewel Lake for at least a year before feeling settled enough to begin to date, because what if she hated it here? Also, if she bounced into a relationship so soon after moving, it would only prove to her parents that she hadn't outgrown the impulsive ways that had contributed to her fling with Connor as a teen.

But she wasn't going to date Blake Cavanagh. There were probably a dozen reasons if she listed them, and she didn't need to give the whimsy so much credence that she'd actually put pen to paper. She wasn't going to date him or anyone else for at least a year. Decision made.

"This is one of my favorite spots on the ranch." Kathryn settled onto a rock near the creek and beckoned to Dafne. "Especially this time of year."

Dafne could see why, but every which way she turned at this elevation, the view was stunning. Golden leaves mottled the evergreen slopes, gleaming in the sunlight. And the smell... it was intoxicating, full of nature at its finest.

She looked for Gavin, but he was right behind her, clinging to Blake's hand. Then he reached for hers, and she couldn't turn her boy away, not even if it meant that he was between her and the cowboy, making them look like a real little family. There was no one to notice or to care, but she'd have a talk with Gavin later.

And say what, exactly? Her problems weren't on her son.

Kathryn looked between the three of them, eyebrows raised slightly as a tiny smile hovered on her lips.

Okay, fine. Blake's stepmother was here. She saw. She noticed. But she'd soon find her notions disabused.

"Come here, Gavin." Kathryn beckoned. "Let's throw sticks in the creek and see where they land up in the pool around the bend."

"Yeah!" Gavin dropped both hands and darted toward Kathryn. A second later they earnestly discussed the best sticks for creek-floating.

Leaving Dafne standing awkwardly a couple of feet from the handsome cowboy she was not going to fall for. She wrapped her arms around her middle.

"You okay? Cold?"

"I'm fine. Thanks." Dafne strode toward her son just as he launched a stick into the middle of the creek, crowing in delight. She clapped. "Nice throw, baby!"

He flashed her a grin and grabbed Kathryn's hand, towing her downstream.

Leaving Dafne with Blake. Again.

The cowboy chuckled. "He's a firecracker, that one."

She turned to look at him, this time from a safe distance. "He's pretty awesome."

The safe distance didn't last as Blake closed it with just a few strides. "Is his dad in the picture?"

Dafne gaped then snapped her mouth shut before pivoting to look back at the creek. "No." If she could send *stop this conversation* vibes, she definitely would.

"Is he from around here? Is that why you moved to Jewel Lake?"

"No. He's from Spokane."

"Were you married to him?"

Why could this cowboy not read her body language and leave her alone? "I was sixteen when I got pregnant. I was certainly not married to him then or ever."

"Is there anyone else?"

Drat the man. Not only was he not catching hints, but he was nearer now. Close enough she could feel the heat of his body behind her. Could smell the honest scent of sweat. Her traitorous mind flashed to the vision of Blake without a shirt. His brother had also been shirtless, but somehow Dafne hadn't really appreciated that so much.

She shifted a few steps away.

"Dafne?" He followed her. Again.

"No one." She lifted her chin, still staring out across the

tumbling water. "And that's how it's going to stay for a while. I've got Gavin to think of."

Blake's strong hands rested on her hips from behind. "I was thinking of him, too."

Dafne whirled away to break the contact. "He's my respon—" She was going to say *responsibility*, but her foot slid off a mossy rock, and her ankle twisted as she flailed to keep her balance. "Ouch."

Again, the cowboy came to her rescue, steadying her, lifting her back onto the solid bank. Hovering.

She sank to the ground and rubbed her left ankle. It just plain hurt. Tears pricked her eyes. Why did she always have to look so needy and incompetent in front of this guy?

Blake knelt in front of her and loosened her shoelace. His warm hands gently probed her ankle. "It's swelling."

Yeah, no doubt. And she was going to have to put weight on it to get back on Lady. And the whole way back to Rockstead she'd be using both feet to stay balanced. She bit back a whimper at the thought. *Buck up. Don't be such a baby.*

"Riding's going to hurt."

Nice observation, Einstein. She nodded.

Gavin's chatter became louder. His and Kathryn's foot-steps crackled in the dry leaves. Blake rocked to his feet.

At least that gave Dafne some air, but it felt chillier than it had a few minutes ago.

"Dafne twisted her ankle on a rock."

Nice of him not to announce she'd been trying to get away from him. That he'd been crowding her. In fact, this was all his fault.

"I don't think she can put weight on it, so why don't you

take Gavin up with you, and I'll take Dafne? I can pony Lady along, no problem."

Oh, no. This was not happening. They were at least an hour's ride from the ranch. She could absolutely not spend that long pressed up against Blake Cavanagh on the back of a horse.

"Lady's big! She's not a pony." Gavin wrapped his arms around Dafne's neck, squeezing her airways.

She tugged him around and into her lap, wincing as she shifted her legs.

"When someone leads another horse, it's called pony-ing." Kathryn lowered herself to sit by Dafne. "You going to be okay? Do I need to call an ambulance for you?"

Dafne managed a smile. Imagine being airlifted off this mountain. "I'll be fine." By next week, for sure.

"Are you okay if I take Gavin with me?"

What choice did she have? It was either bend to Blake's dictates or be in a ton more pain when she finally rode into the Rockstead corral under her own steam.

This way, the pain was bound to be in her heart. She braced herself and nodded. "Sure. Thanks."

"I'M TOO HEAVY." Dafne backed away from Zorro.

"It's fine. He's strong." Blake looped Lady's reins to the back of the saddle. "I wouldn't suggest it if it would be too hard for him."

"But…" She bit her lip and looked at Blake then back at the horse.

"Granted, two adult riders isn't ideal for any horse, but Zorro is up for it for this short of a distance. The alternative is going to cause you more pain than this will cause him. He's big and strong."

She glanced down the trail, but Kathryn had already disappeared with Gavin.

"Dafne." He kept his voice as level as possible.

"What?"

"You're afraid."

She shook her head swiftly, but that did nothing to convince him.

"You're either afraid of pain, or you're afraid of me."

Heaven knew, that ought to be reciprocated. Blake should be terrified of the woman in front of him. She'd gotten under his skin in a way no one else ever had. Not Felicity, or Marnie, or Arlene. Not any of the women who'd come before them. No matter how many times he'd told himself how very *not* suitable Dafne was for him, she'd wiggled her way into his life. Her and that cute kid of hers.

Dafne straightened. "I'm not afraid."

"Prove it."

She closed her eyes for a second then limped forward.

Blake didn't wait for a clearer invitation. He simply put his hands on her waist and lifted her to Zorro's saddle with no further ado.

Dafne gasped, but the deed was done, and she was up there.

"I'll sit behind you, so scoot forward."

There wasn't a ton of extra room, but they could make it work, and it would be far more fun than not. Who was he trying to kid? It was going to be heaven, but then it would end. Blake's motto had always been to enjoy the moment and not worry about later. It was even scriptural. *Tomorrow will worry about itself. Each day has enough trouble of its own.* Or something like that.

Nestling Dafne against his chest as he settled into the saddle was definitely trouble. He glanced back at Lady then touched Zorro's flanks lightly as he clicked his tongue. "Gid up."

Zorro shifted into a smooth walk, and Dafne swayed against Blake's chest.

His left hand held the reins, and he tucked his right arm around her. After all, he needed someplace to put it, and she seemed to need the security.

She stiffened. Tried to sit without leaning on him.

"It's easier if you relax."

"Relax? That's impossible."

He kind of agreed. Every nerve ending leaned toward Dafne, and they were touching in a lot of places. Awareness hummed through him. "Try." He was talking to himself as much as her.

"I don't even like you, you know."

Blake chuckled at her unexpected words. "That makes one of us."

"You mean you like yourself."

"I mean, I like you. I promise I didn't want to."

"You don't even know me."

"I know enough to be intrigued. Enough to want to know more."

She shook her head against his chest, her hair brushing his cheek. "I'm not that interesting. I'm a girl who messed up her life as a teenager. A girl whose parents had to bail her out of all kinds of trouble and babysit a newborn right when they thought they'd be empty-nesters. A girl who was so focused on grades all through college she didn't get out much. A girl who's determined to make restitution."

"Want to know what I see?" Blake didn't wait for her to answer, because she'd probably say no. "I see a woman who's possibly a little more independent than she needs to be, but who's also loyal and responsible. Who's raised an amazing, inquisitive kid. Who—"

She snorted.

"What? You don't think Gavin is amazing?" Better to go with that than to linger on the other.

"He chatters incessantly. You can't tell me inquisitive-ness is a good quality."

"Oh, but it is. He's bright and curious. Someone who's willing and eager to learn about everything around them will go far."

"My dad can only handle so many questions at a time."

Blake filed the information away. "I bet Gavin misses his grandfather." Sounded like the man was nothing like Declan. No kid would miss Declan.

"He does. My parents keep after me to come for the weekend."

A weekend without Dafne and Gavin in it? Blake didn't want to think about it. "You probably should sometime before the snow flies. Those are some high passes heading into Idaho. Do you have good tires?"

"Now you sound like my brother. Peter took my car for new ones before I moved. Said it was my birthday present."

"I think I like your brother." But would Dafne's brother

like *him*? That was the bigger question, and the answer was probably negative.

But why did it matter? It didn't. Right?

Wrong. He'd already gone out on a limb and admitted to her that he liked her. And that wasn't a proclamation he expected to retract anytime soon.

CHAPTER ELEVEN

She really needed to make some friends in Jewel Lake that weren't Cavanaghs or attached to them, because here she was in church beside Ainsley, with Nathaniel then Noah beyond. Dakota and Travis sat toward the back, and Kathryn sat a few rows closer to the front with Ryder on one side and Adam and Riley on the other.

Dafne had met Riley once. She and Adam lived in one of the little cabins on Rockstead. Dafne hadn't seen the inside of one of those, but they didn't seem that much bigger than the trappers cabin. Maybe double, which was still tiny for a family, not that Riley and Adam had any kids. They both worked on the ranch, Blake said, sometimes together and sometimes on different tasks.

That was no way to live, especially not with Declan Cavanagh for a boss. The man scared Dafne. Not causing her nightmares — not that kind of fear — just someone she didn't want to be around any more than required. Since he didn't attend church and didn't hang out at Ainsley's or at Kathryn's, he was fairly avoidable.

If Dafne quit accepting invitations to Rockstead Ranch, she could dodge him completely. Blake, too. Did she want to? It would be a whole lot safer than lingering near his flame. She'd been scorched last time she'd played with fire.

She felt Blake looming over the end of the pew before she saw or heard him.

"This spot taken?"

There wasn't really room, but she already knew he didn't care about personal space.

Ainsley scooted closer to Nathaniel. "Sure. We can make room."

Blake raised his eyebrows at Dafne, a grin playing at the corners of his mouth.

Yeah, she was in desperate need of non-Cavanagh friends. She edged toward Ainsley, and Blake wedged himself in beside her, the length of him warming her side.

"Hey, good morning." He nudged her arm. Or maybe that was simply all the room there was. "How's your ankle?"

"Better." Dafne focused on the front of the church as the worship team took their places.

"Welcome to Creekside Fellowship." The guy on the platform strummed his guitar. "Let me call you to worship this morning from Psalm 96. 'Sing to the Lord a new song; sing to the Lord, all the earth. Sing to the Lord, praise his name; proclaim his salvation day after day. Declare his glory among the nations, his marvelous deeds among all peoples. For great is the Lord and most worthy of praise; he is to be feared above all gods.'"

This wasn't Bridgeview Bible Church, where Dafne had attended her entire life, but it was good. This guy wasn't Logan Dermott, but Caleb led well. It wasn't Pastor Tomas preaching, but Pastor Marshall Smith was also insightful.

There was a youth pastor, too, who taught some of the academy's Bible classes. Dafne had seen him out her window a couple of times shooting hoops with some of the students.

This was a good church with solid teaching and people of all ages and stages of life. Gavin loved his morning class like he had back home. This was home now. She could settle into it.

Though it would have been easier if Blake Cavanagh wasn't squished against her side. If he hadn't told her he liked her yesterday. Who said they 'liked' a girl? Wasn't that for schoolkids? And yet it had warmed her, possibly too much, and it was a start. Better than the false start they'd had, back in the Copper Carafe.

Everyone around her stood. She'd been daydreaming and missed her cue, so she rose now, leaning on her right foot, as the first song, an old hymn she'd known all her life, came up on the screen.

"Oh, Lord, my God, when I in awesome wonder consider all the works Thy hands have made. I see the stars; I hear the rolling thunder. Thy power throughout the universe displayed. Then sings my soul, my Savior, God, to Thee: how great Thou art. How great Thou art. Then sings my soul, my Savior, God, to Thee: how great Thou art. How great Thou art."

Blake sang out with a strong, solid tenor. On the other side, Ainsley had a great voice, too. Dafne joined in, tentatively at first, but she couldn't conquer the final 'how great Thou art' in the chorus without a little more gusto.

"When through the woods, and forest glades I wander, I hear the birds sing sweetly in the trees…"

Dafne closed her eyes and remembered the 'lofty mountain grandeur' she'd seen just yesterday from the cabin. There'd been a glimpse of Glacier National Park way up the valley, and her heart had been full from observing God's magnificent creation.

Her heart had been full of Blake, too. Why wouldn't he catch a hint? Didn't he realize she wasn't good for him? She definitely knew he wasn't good for her. Not a guy who had a reputation around town as a playboy. How on earth had she attracted the attention of someone like him? She didn't think she'd been giving off the easy vibe for the past seven years, not since Connor, but Blake was still here, right beside her, acting for all the world like they belonged together.

Connor never darkened the door of a church back home. The only time she'd seen him inside was at his brother's wedding to Dafne's cousin. She couldn't imagine Connor singing out. Couldn't imagine him listening carefully to the preacher like Blake did, now that they were seated again.

Blake glanced sideways and caught her watching him. He winked and crossed his arms, which only had the effect of pressing even tighter against her shoulder, before looking back at the platform.

No, Blake was not Connor. He might have a related reputation, but at the core, the two guys could not be more different.

That didn't mean she was safe with Blake, though. Anything but. He made her feel aware and alive, dangerously alive.

Maybe she really ought to sit down and make an itemized list of all the reasons he was bad for her. She'd had a whole bunch of them at the tip of her tongue just a few days ago. It would do her good to get them down, ink on paper, so she could repeat and affirm them.

Problem was, right now, sitting in church wedged between him and Ainsley, Dafne couldn't remember a single one.

He liked her. He was good with Gavin. He was a Christian, or, at least, he was comfortable inside a Bible-preaching church.

Her reasons fluttered away like so many yellow leaves off a tree in autumn.

AT THE END of the service, Blake turned to Dafne. "Do you have plans for lunch? You and Gavin should join us at the Golden Grill. They push a bunch of tables together for our crew on Sundays."

She looked at him, startled, her mouth slightly open.

He could kiss that mouth. But not here. Not now, even though he was seated, and her fancy moves wouldn't splat him on the floor. He couldn't help grinning at her with the thought.

"I can—"

"Great. Toby will be excited to see Gavin."

"I was saying I *can't*."

Couldn't or wouldn't? Not much difference at the moment. "Sure, you can. Everyone needs to eat, and the Grill puts on a great spread. Have you been yet?"

Ainsley leaned from Dafne's other side. "Why not? It's an awesome idea. I love their Reuben on rye."

Dafne straightened just enough Blake felt the movement against his arm more than he saw it. "No, thank you. Not this week."

He'd pushed too much. Or Ainsley had. But he still couldn't let it go. Couldn't let *her* go. "Aw, c'mon. I'll pick up your tab." Maybe he should have led with that. He'd planned to, anyway, but maybe she'd been so broke as a single mom that she never ate out. Coffee at the Copper Carafe notwithstanding.

She rose and looked down at him. "*No* is a complete sentence all on its own. I don't need to explain."

Blake stared. That was certainly true, but...

"She's got you there, Blake." Ainsley chuckled.

Nathaniel's fiancée should keep her opinions to herself. Women hadn't turned him down very often, not until recently. Felicity then Marnie had forcefully ditched him. He'd managed to do the deed with Arlene... wait. She'd accused him of breaking up so that he was the one in control for once. Could Arlene have been right? Because he definitely didn't like being on the rejection end. This called for a regroup and a rethink. "Sorry." He drawled out the second syllable.

"Excuse me, please." Dafne pointed at his knees, which blocked her exit.

The old Blake would have snagged her around the waist and pulled her into his lap, absolutely certain this was what she wanted. The newly reformed Blake was a lot less confident. He should probably respect her words — at least, if he ever wanted to prove he wasn't going to give up easily.

He rose and stepped into the aisle, then dipped his head and gestured her forward.

"Thank you." And she limped toward the back of the sanctuary, her pretty blue dress accentuating her narrow waist and floating around her knees.

"Blake?"

He turned slowly to look at his stepbrothers. Both Nathaniel and Noah had risen and looked at him with amusement on their faces. They might be twins, but they weren't identical, no matter how similar their expressions were in the moment.

"Excuse me. I need to get Bella from the nursery." Ainsley darted away, leaving Blake with the guys.

"Whatever you're thinking, it's not that." Sometimes bluffing worked.

The twins exchanged an unspoken conversation.

"Is your backside still sore enough to get even with her?"

Blake had forgotten Noah had witnessed the incident in the coffee shop. "My tailbone has recovered just fine, thanks."

"It's his ego that hasn't." Nathaniel smirked. "He's still got something to prove."

"Not true. Have you ever thought of the possibility that I actually wanted to hang out with her?" The words were no sooner out of his mouth than he realized what he'd admitted. Not to just anyone, but to this pair who didn't even need words to communicate with each other.

He'd hated that as a kid. They were less than a year older than he was, but there'd never been room for him in their twosome. Travis and Adam had been rivals with never any love lost between them. But Blake with Kathryn's twins? There'd been no way to contend. They were twins. He was outside. The end. No wonder he'd gone his own way. He had stuff to prove.

"The girls think she's really nice," offered Noah.

Blake blinked. No egging? That was a switch. And good for Noah, hanging out with their younger sisters and actually listening to them.

"She's a good friend to Ainsley, too." Nathaniel poked Blake's arm. "Watch your step with her, is all."

"Hey! Whose side are you on? I'm your bro. You should be telling *her* not to break my tender heart."

Noah snapped his fingers at Nathaniel. "What's that scripture?"

"The one about the heart of stone?"

"Yeah."

"Somewhere in Ezekiel, I think."

"Something about God removing Israel's heart of stone and replacing it with a new heart, a heart of flesh."

"Oh, give up. My heart is not a rock."

Nathaniel's eyebrows shot up. "All evidence to the contrary?"

"What is this, pick on Blake day? Dafne did a good enough job of that. She doesn't need any help flattening me."

"That's for sure." Noah's laugh belted out. Good thing nearly everyone had left the sanctuary by now, though

Caleb Grant was still on stage, tucking his guitar into its case. He glanced over with a questioning grin.

Okay, fine. Blake hadn't even been thinking of the physical takedown. She'd done it to his body, yes. And she'd done it to his hopes, to his spirit, several times. Like two minutes ago. Was he some kind of glutton for punishment who needed to keep coming back for more?

Not him. Not Blake Daniel Cavanagh. He pivoted and strode toward the back of the church, dodging through the crowd, not pausing to greet anyone. He heard someone call his name, but he was done here.

And, no, he wasn't going to the Golden Grill for lunch with his brothers. He'd had enough of the lot of them.

He needed a place to lick his wounds and figure out what he really wanted from life.

Did he want Dafne, really? Or was it just the thrill of the chase and saving face from that day in the coffee shop?

How should he know?

Blake jabbed the key into his truck's ignition, started it, and peeled out of the parking lot.

CHAPTER TWELVE

Fourteen teens looked back at Dafne. Five weeks into the school year, this wasn't nearly as intimidating as it had been at first.

She also had a little less to prove. For the first time, she wore pants to class. Her ankle wasn't going to last the day in even low heels, and her flats didn't look that great with a skirt. Or, maybe Montana was rubbing off on her.

"Tell me what you know about Montana becoming a state." She perched on the corner of her desk and looked around. "Who's got something?"

Emma's hand shot up. "It happened in 1889."

"That's right. Who knows what Montana was like before that?"

"Everyone flocked here because of the gold rush, and my great-great-grandfather began ranching to supply beef for the camps. And, when the railroad came, they started sending beef east, too." Emma looked around. Everyone was staring at her except her twin, who'd slumped dramatically in her seat. "What?"

Didn't sound like there was much Dafne, a native Washingtonian, could teach these kids about Montana history. She should just call Emma Cavanagh up front and turn her loose. Hmm.

"That's really interesting, Emma. I'd like to start in the back of the room, and each of you tell the class when you or your ancestors came to Montana. If you know why they moved here, tell us that, too. Josh?"

The boy's shoulders drooped. "We moved from Minneapolis two years ago because my dad got a job with the town."

Okay, so not everyone had been here forever. "Lance?"

"My great-grandparents came after the second world war. He was a teacher at the high school in Missoula."

"Rory?"

The boy shrugged. "They came on a wagon train, I think. I don't really know."

"Jake?"

"Forever, I bet." He rolled his eyes.

"Okay, I think we have a project." Dafne walked around her desk, trying not to wince when she put weight on her left foot. "I'd like everyone to do some research this week and write a paper—"

Groans chorused from around the room.

"—about your family history in this state. I'd like you to come up with at least five hundred words." She eyed Emma. "And no more two thousand. If you have some photos you can scan and bring to show everyone, that would be great."

Some smart-mouth from the back made a comment

about kindergarten show-and-tell. Jake? Dafne wasn't sure, so she ignored him.

"This assignment will be due next Monday."

Alexia glared at Emma. The teen wouldn't try to slide in with her twin's work, would she? Emma was smarter than to allow that.

"Ms. Santoro?" Elsie waved her hand. "I'm adopted."

Dafne should have thought of that. The twins had told her their friend had been adopted from China as a child. "Then you're welcome to tell either your own story, or about your adoptive family. Whichever you prefer."

"Okay."

"Anyone else have any questions?" Dafne glanced at the clock, hoping none of the teens noticed. This was the Mondayest Monday she'd ever endured. She'd blame it on her ankle, but Blake Cavanagh was as much responsible. Not only had he caused her stumble up in the mountains, but her thoughts were tumbling all over the place, too.

She focused on Emma and Alexia. Today was for teaching teenagers, not for daydreaming about the cowboy who wouldn't seem to stay out of her head, no matter how many times she removed him.

And… again.

The kids stared back, shifting restlessly in their seats.

"Okay, it's five minutes to the bell, so why don't you grab a paper and start jotting down notes of what you know about your family's history? If you think of some questions to ask your parents or grandparents, write those down, too."

The Cavanagh twins leaned close to each other and whispered.

Should Dafne insist on focus and quiet? Everyone else seemed to be preparing for the assignment. She approached their table. "Everything okay?" she asked quietly.

Emma looked up with pleading eyes. "Can one of us do our dad's family and the other our mom's?"

"Sure. That sounds like a great idea." And, just like that, Dafne realized she was going to learn a lot about Blake Cavanagh's background, too. At least from the history of Declan's side of the family.

Also, she'd need to rethink this paper if she decided to assign it to the Senior class, too. What would Vivienne Johnson write about? She was the twins' half-sister — Declan's daughter — though she'd only met her father for the first time a couple of months ago from what Ainsley said.

Dafne knew better than to create this type of home-work. Her own family had been the traditional all-American family: Dad, Mom, and three kids. She kept forgetting that not everyone had had a similar idyllic situation. She'd learned about it in her college classes and in her practice teaching, and it certainly played out in Gavin's life, but it was still hard to remember. These kids might all come from Christian homes with enough wealth for private school, but that didn't mean their families were anything like hers.

Did that mean she shouldn't create assignments about their personal histories? No. Those were significant and relevant. She just needed to make sure the parameters were loose enough to allow for all of her students to complete it, one way or another.

She limped over to the other table. "Hey, Elsie, can you see how to make this assignment work for you?"

The girl tapped her pencil against the table and pursed her lips. "I remember the orphanage and coming to America on the plane with my new parents."

"I'd feel really honored to read about that experience, and what your impressions were. How old were you?"

"Eight."

Dafne nodded. She remembered tons of stuff from that age. Ava turning thirteen and all the drama that had caused in the family's life. Peter as a teen, taking basketball as seriously as he took grades. Her parents encouraging all three to make a plan for their lives that included following Jesus every day.

Elsie flashed her a shy smile. "Thanks, Ms. Santoro."

"You're welcome. I look forward to your paper."

The boys at the back table started elbowing each other just as the bell rang.

Whew. Another class over. One more until she could pick up Gavin, go home, and wrap her sore ankle in an ice pack.

"*FINE!* MARCH FIRST, THEN."

Blake's boots welded to the passageway in the stable at his father's voice, nearly pitching him face-first in the horse muck. Whose task was stable cleanup this week? Huh. Probably his. He missed having his twin sisters living on the ranch.

"December first." Adam's voice.

"I need you here for calving."

"Running Creek is right next door. Not too far for the truck, the ATV, or a horse."

Enlightenment flooded Blake. Ah... the whole topic of Kathryn's sons wanting ownership — or at least access — to the ranch Joe and Kathryn had owned before Kathryn married his dad and moved to Rockstead. Whatever had happened to the deed for Running Creek in that business transaction — because the parental units had hardly married for love — had never been clearly disclosed to any of the boys.

Adam was Joe Anderson's firstborn. He'd been pushing for his parents' homeplace to be turned over to him and his twin brothers ever since he'd quit the rodeo and come home a couple of years back. He'd even pretended to be engaged to Riley in the belief that would add weight to his claim.

Blake choked back a chuckle. That had backfired in two ways. One, it turned out Riley and Adam actually had been in love but were scared to tell each other, and two, their bluff had infuriated Dad. Which admittedly didn't take much. Listen to him growling right now.

"Adam's right. There are options."

Travis?

Blake leaned against the gate to Zorro's pen, dug a carrot out of his pocket for the gelding, and settled in to listen. Travis had threatened to quit cowboying for Dad a few weeks ago. He hadn't really meant it, had he?

"It's my ranch. You work for me."

"Until we don't. Look, I'm thirty. All us guys are responsible, adult human beings. Even Blake."

Hey, now. That ought to be enough to rile him up, but mostly, Blake was curious where this was all going.

"You're not quitting on me. Ranching is in your blood. My great-grandfather settled this land over a hundred and fifty years ago. You're not walking away from a legacy like that. Neither of you."

"I think it's time to lay out a plan for transition, Dad. Not just for Adam and his brothers with Running Creek, but for all six of us on both spreads. We need to know where we stand."

"And the girls," Adam added. "They're your kids, too."

"All three of them."

Dad snarled like a cornered mountain lion. Maybe it was time Blake showed himself, because his brothers were not wrong. He always felt he was just one misstep away from needing a job on some other ranch. What else could a guy like him do? Dad was right. Ranching ran through his veins, and he didn't have the education to pursue anything else.

A man couldn't let his wife support him and their family. Teachers didn't make that much.

He blinked. Teachers? Why did Dafne come to mind when he thought of the future? Hadn't he always said he wasn't going to settle down? He had… but surely he hadn't meant it. Think of growing old like Dad, rattling around in that big house by himself now that his second wife had walked out.

Only Blake would just have the little cabin by the creek, next to his brothers', not a big house. Nope. He wanted more. A wife. Kids. An actual home.

He rubbed Zorro's cheek, whispered a prayer, and walked around the corner into the tack room.

All three men pivoted and looked at him.

Blake nodded slowly, meeting Travis's gaze, then Adam's, then Dad's. "A transition plan sounds like a good idea. There's got to be an attorney in Jewel Lake or Missoula who specializes in that sort of thing."

"You kids expect everything handed to you on a silver platter. I had to work for all this."

"We haven't worked?" Travis's eyebrows shot up.

"You didn't have five brothers." Blake kept his tone as mild as possible. "You knew where you stood in the hierarchy."

"Good point." His brother nodded. "It would have been different if Callum had lived."

The boys had heard the story of how Dad's younger brother had been lost in a flash flood while herding cattle.

"You boys are bluffing."

Heart pounding, Blake shook his head. If all six of them stayed strong together, Dad would have to make changes or hire a bunch of rookie cowboys who didn't know better. He'd never let it come to that. Would he?

"Not a bit of it." Travis stood tall, thumbs tucked through his belt loops. "If I'm going to need a different job, I'd like to get started on it sooner rather than later. I told you months ago, Dakota and I want to build a house down on the bend and move onto the ranch. All respect to Adam, but I'm not asking *my* wife to live in one of those little shacks by the creek."

"Which brings me back to Running Creek," Adam said. "Riley and I want to start a family, but not while living in what's basically a bunkhouse. December first gives you a solid sixty days to give notice to the renters. And it will allow Riley and me to have Christmas in an actual home."

Blake shifted a little closer to his brothers and mimicked their stance.

"You think Nathaniel and Ryder won't stand with us?" Travis asked. "Even Noah. He's been rumbling a bit here and there about wishing he had a place to settle down. Getting tired of being a circuit-riding farrier."

He had? Blake hadn't heard. He hadn't paid a whole lot of attention to what was going on his brothers' lives. He'd just tucked his chin down, completed his assigned tasks, and spent the rest of his time off the ranch, as far from Dad as possible.

Avoidance at its finest. Acting like he was seventeen instead of twenty-seven. Even Dafne, four years younger than him, had a degree and a plan for her life. A plan that didn't include a laze-about like him.

Could he blame her? There wasn't much in him to attract a woman with an eye on the future. He might be good-looking — enough women had told him so that he had to believe it, and his mirror didn't lie — but it was just skin-deep. If he wanted to settle down someday, he needed to grow up. Be purposeful. Make decisions like he meant them instead of floating at the whim of the current like a stick tossed into a creek by a six-year-old.

Blake nodded at Travis. "Our other brothers will agree. I'd like to see a plan in place, myself. Someday I'll want to get hitched, too, and... I just don't know how to plan, with everything up in the air like this. Travis already lives in town. Nathaniel's going to when he and Ainsley get married. Pretty soon none of us will live at Rockstead."

"Whoa. What?" Adam pivoted to gawk at him. "You're thinking of marriage? Who's the lucky girl? Last I heard—"

"Never mind what you heard or what you think you saw." Blake narrowed his gaze at his stepbrother. "That's not the point here. The point is transition planning."

"Right. But after that, I expect you to spill."

Travis elbowed Adam and grinned at Blake. "Get in line, bro. I need to hear this confession, too."

CHAPTER THIRTEEN

Seth had a Global Sunbeams conference in Vegas, Eliza has the girls, so here we are."

Shock forgotten, Dafne dashed into her sister's arms for a big squeeze. "I can't believe you drove all this way without telling me!" She plucked her two-year-old nephew from Ava's hip and spun him around. "Leo!"

"Daffin!" he squealed.

Gavin charged down the short hallway. "Auntie Ava! Leo! Mama didn't tell me you were coming to see us."

Ava scooped up Gavin. "That's because it was a surprise for both of you. Do you like your surprise?"

"Yes!" He peered past her to the car at the curb. "Are Nonna and Nonni here, too?"

"No, bug. Just Leo and me this time."

Dafne dragged her sister inside and shut the door. "Why didn't you call? Give a girl some warning! What if I hadn't been home?"

Ava raised an eyebrow. "Where were you going to go, since you adamantly told Mom you had too much grading to do? Seriously, Daf, somebody needed to come check on you. We've missed you heaps and piles and mountains, and it feels like you're avoiding all of us."

Tears prickled Dafne's eyes. "That's not it at all. You know better. I'm just trying to be a responsible adult and create a home for Gavin and me. I can't be dragging him back and forth every weekend, so he doesn't even know where we really live."

"Daf. You don't need to try to be a responsible adult. You *are* one. And wherever you are is where Gavin's home is."

Dafne dashed the tears from her face. "Thanks. That means a lot. But I did have marking to do. Just because music and dance teachers don't give pop quizzes and assign papers doesn't mean social studies teachers don't."

Ava rolled her eyes. "I do so give pop quizzes. But you're right. It is different. How do you like your job? Tell me everything."

That could wait. "I can't believe you're here!"

"I brought a blow-up mattress just in case. And Leo's pack-and-play, of course. We need to head back Sunday after church. You do go to church, don't you?"

"Of course, I do. Creekside Fellowship is across the parking lot from the academy. It's not quite the same as Bridgeview Bible, but it's pretty good. Gavin loves the kids' program."

Her son had dragged his little cousin off into his bedroom. Hopefully he'd remembered about tiny toys like Legos. He'd been good about it with Bella the times Ainsley had brought her over.

Ava curled up in the corner of the sofa and tucked her feet under her. "Any cute cowboys?"

"This is Montana. There's no shortage of cowboys."

"Oh?" Ava tilted her head to one side. "Any in particular?"

"Sis, I'm not looking. You know that. I've got Gav—"

"Ms. Responsible. You're a grownup, Daf. You're allowed to date. Haven't we had this conversation before? The right guy is going to fall hard for you and Gavin both. Although I hope he's not a cowboy."

Dafne tried to push Blake Cavanagh out of her head, but the obstinate man planted his cowboy boots and crossed his arms, grinning at her. "Why's that?"

"That would mean you'd live on a ranch out here and never move back to Bridgeview."

"I think you need to accept that I don't live there anymore. I needed to stretch my wings and—"

"And then come home in two or three years. Right?"

Dafne shook her head. "That's not the plan. This is a great place. I have a terrific job with great students."

"But—"

"This is why I didn't tell you or Mom or Dad until it was a done deal. I need this, Ava. I know you're happy living in Bridgeview, and that's great for you. But I needed something different."

"Generation Z moves every few years. There's nothing to say you can't come back when you're ready."

"Then there's nothing to say you and Seth can't move away. Like to Jewel Lake."

"Except that Global Sunbeams is paying for his degree at WSU."

Right. Dafne shrugged and tilted her head in concession.

Ava and Seth were stuck in Spokane for the next few years unless they wanted to take on that financial burden themselves. And why would they? Seth had been offered a great opportunity, and he loved his job. Ava loved hers. They had custody of Seth's young half-sisters, but the girls' aunt lived in the other half of the duplex and was very involved in their lives. None of that crew was leaving Bridgeview any minute soon.

"Can we not argue about this all weekend? I want to enjoy your visit and not fight."

Ava leaned over and gave Dafne an impulsive hug. "Sure. So long as you remember that nothing about this has to be permanent unless you make it that way."

"Ava."

Her sister raised both hands. "Okay, okay. Now, what's there to do in this town? The lake looked pretty when I came down the hill into town. The leaves are golden all around it. Very few trees are turning back home."

"We're at like twice the elevation of Spokane."

"That's crazy."

"Still true."

Ava shuddered. "You're going to get a nasty winter here."

"No worse than Spokane, from what I hear. I can easily walk to work and even the grocery store. It's great that Gavin's daycare is in the same building as the academy, so we can walk together."

"That does sound ideal. And I know you have good tires."

"Peter made sure of that."

Ava chuckled. "That's what big brothers are for."

"Direct quote." Dafne laughed, too. "Hey, can I make us a cup of tea or something? Or do you want to go out and see the town now?"

Ava surged to her feet. "Let's go exploring. I'll change Leo first. There are sidewalks, right? I brought his stroller."

"I'm not sure what kind of hick town you thought I'd moved to. Yes, there are sidewalks, as you may have noticed along the street when you parked."

"It *is* the Wild West. I was just checking."

Dafne rolled her eyes as she followed Ava to Gavin's room. It was good to see her sister.

BLAKE PULLED into the Super One lot and parked on the outer edge. He sighed at the multitude of vehicles. Everyone in town must be here. Imagine him on domestic duty, but Cook had asked for a volunteer to pick up the weekly grocery order, and he'd agreed. Why not? It wasn't like he had a social life anymore. Though he wanted to, if the woman was Dafne.

He gave his head a shake as he jumped out of the truck. At first, he'd tried to tell himself his attraction was only because he wasn't used to being turned away without a bit of flirtation to soften the blow. Then, somehow, the attraction had become a fixation. Not in a negative sense... right? It was just that he found himself thinking about her at random times. Okay, not random. Pretty much constantly.

Like now. It was Saturday noon, and he wondered what she was having for lunch. He'd never once been curious what Felicity or Marnie or Arlene ate when he wasn't around. Why should he think about Dafne? Except he cared about everything she did.

He double-tapped his key fob, listened for the lock to beep, and turned toward the supermarket. Cook had told him to check with customer service, and someone would bring the order out to the truck and help him load it.

A child pushing a baby stroller careened around the street corner, the toddler strapped within squealing in glee as the contraption hovered on two wheels rather than four. Some people let their kids — wait. That was Dafne's boy!

Blake settled his cowboy hat on his head and strode closer. "Hey, Gavin. Careful with the baby." At first, he'd thought the little one might be Bella, but no. The somber brown eyes of a boy stared back at him, his lower lip trembling.

"Hi, Mr. Blake! This is my cousin, and he likes going fast."

Cousin? Blake glanced around just as Dafne rounded the corner, deep in conversation with a woman who looked a lot like her, except her dark hair was wound into a knot on top of her head while Dafne's was tied into a low ponytail.

"Dafne? Hi." He swept the hat off his head and nodded to her, glancing between the two of them.

Her face flushed instantly as she looked at the other woman and then back to him. She took a deep breath. "Hi, Blake. I'd like you to meet my sister, Ava. She's visiting from Spokane for the weekend with her little boy, Leo.

Ava, Blake's mom is one of the other teachers I've been working with. And, uh, he's the brother of some of my students."

He chuckled. He couldn't help it. She was certainly going out of her way to categorize their friendship — they had one, didn't they? — in a way that would keep her sister from guessing the sparks that zinged between them. She might try to deny it, but that didn't stop it from being true.

"Blake?" The other woman extended her hand. "I'm Ava Donahue, and I'm so pleased to meet you."

"Likewise." Wow, Ava had a strong grip. If there was any message in that, it was alleviated by her amused smile. That was reassuring. Maybe.

"What's fun to do around here, Blake?" Ava reached for the stroller handles but kept her gaze on him. "My sister hasn't been here that long, and she doesn't seem to have gotten out much. Any kid-friendly tips?"

"Ava!" Dafne's voice was low, but the warning was clear.

"What, Daf? I know it's not Spokane, so I doubt there's a children's museum, but there must be something to do both boys would enjoy."

Normally Blake might suggest a hike up Miner's Rock on the bluff across the lake, but the trail wasn't exactly made for strollers. He scratched his head and replaced his hat. "I'm not really sure, ma'am, not having a little one myself. But there's always horseback riding, if you're up for it."

"Yes!" Gavin hopped in a circle, pumping his fist.

At least Blake had one fan.

"I've never been on a horse in my life."

"It's up to Dafne, of course, but she's been riding a few times now."

She stiffened, and he cut off his smirk. She was going to make him pay for that revelation, he could tell, but it would be worth it. Anything that got her near him for a while was worth the price.

Ava smacked her sister's arm. "You didn't even tell me! Was it fun?"

"Has your ankle healed?" Blake kept his voice innocent. "If so, you all could come up to the ranch this afternoon, and we could take a ride up to the high pastures. I don't think there's time to get all the way up to the trappers cabin and back this time."

"Your ankle?" Ava looked confused. "The *what* cabin?"

Gavin grabbed Dafne's hand and swung it. "Can we, Mama? Maybe I could ride Toby's pony this time. I'd be good at it, Mr. Blake. I've been riding lots of times now, right?"

Ava's eyebrows shot up. "Wow. It sounds like we really should take this guy up on his offer, Daf. Don't you think?"

"The twins are home for the weekend, so I won't saddle Desiree or Domino for you and your sister. But Lady's available, and I know Kathryn wouldn't mind if you rode Laire." He looked at the two little boys. He'd have to put the toddler up with him. Blake crouched in front of Gavin. "You can ride Clover if you listen to everything I tell you."

He wasn't prepared for the little guy to launch at him. Gavin's arms tightened around Blake's neck, and his bony shoulder dug into Blake's throat, cutting off all oxygen while knocking his cowboy hat to the ground. "Thank you, Mr. Blake. I'll listen. I promise."

"I'm sure you will, squirt. But your mama gets to make the final decision." Still squatting on the sidewalk with his arm looped around the boy's middle, he resettled his cowboy hat and looked up at Dafne.

The look she gave him nearly took his breath away. It wasn't as murderous as he'd expected. Instead, it brimmed with longing in the brief instant before she schooled her expression.

Blake's heart leaped. She felt as he did, no matter that she denied it. She'd come around. He just needed to be patient and stay focused. "What do you say, Dafne? I'm here to pick up the grocery order for the ranch, but I can be ready to head back in probably twenty minutes." He hesitated, then went for it. "Or, if you haven't had lunch yet, we could grab something at the Golden Grill before we go. My treat."

Ava turned to Dafne. "Isn't that where you said we were going for lunch?"

Blake rose, picking up Gavin with him. The kid grabbed for his hat again, but this time Blake caught his hand in time. "Have a heart, squirt."

Indecision warred on Dafne's face.

Blake almost felt sorry for cornering her. He'd rather she wanted to be with him than that she felt trapped by him. He opened his mouth to tell her never mind, maybe another time, when she met his gaze.

"Okay. Thanks."

Gavin pumped his fist.

It took everything in Blake not to mimic the little tyke.

CHAPTER FOURTEEN

Ava didn't even wait until she was buckled into the drivers' seat to begin the barrage. "How did I not know you'd been horseback riding with that hunky cowboy a *bunch* of times? That Gavin knows him so well that Blake even has a nickname for him?"

"Shh." Dafne glanced into the backseat as she clipped her own seatbelt. Gavin dug through Leo's toy bag and offered the toddler a board book. Maybe he wasn't paying attention. "Let's not talk about this right now."

"So long as we talk about it later because, girl, you're going to spill."

And this is why Dafne should have gone home for a weekend instead of holding out until her observant sister crashed into her new life. It would have been much easier to pretend her attraction to Blake didn't exist if no one could watch them interact.

Ava shifted the car into gear. "How do I get to this ranch?"

"Back toward the Interstate."

"Okay. I remember that part." She glanced in the mirror and lowered her voice. "Daf, that guy is *hot* for you."

"Aves. Leave it. Someone hears everything."

"He's busy. Trust me. If you're determined to live here, why wouldn't you give that cowboy the time of day? Unless he's not a Christian?"

Dafne closed her eyes and willed her sister to shut up, but of course, it didn't happen.

"You said his family is involved in your private school, so that means he knows about the Lord, at least. Right?"

"We haven't talked about it, but he does go to church." And sing like he meant the words.

"Why not see where it goes?"

She thumbed into the backseat. "That's why."

"Because he doesn't need a father figure? You're not holding out for Connor, are you?"

Dafne pivoted in her seat and glared at her sister. "Are you kidding me? Connor signed off all rights. He's a jerk and an idiot, and he's never coming back into our life."

"Okay, okay. Which way do I go here?"

"Left. The road climbs up beside the lake. There's a nice lookout at the top."

"I'm hoping Leo will have a little nap while we drive, so I'd rather not stop unless you really want to."

What Dafne really wanted was to go back to her condo, watch a movie, and eat popcorn. Or brownies. Or kiss Blake.

Wait. Not that.

Except yes, but she couldn't give in to that urge. Last time she'd gotten pregnant. Okay, it hadn't been from kissing. She wasn't that dumb. But things had spiraled rather quickly from the kissing, and she hadn't been half as attracted to Connor as she was to Blake.

This cowboy was dangerous. She'd been scorched by a firecracker, and Blake was a raging forest fire in comparison.

Ava navigated the turn up the highway out of Jewel Lake. "Promise me you'll give him a real shot."

"But…"

"I'm serious. You deserve happiness, Daf. He's obviously crazy about you. The dude barely took his eyes off you for a second over lunch at that cute retro café. Promise me you'll see where it goes."

"There are a few reasons. The main one is sitting behind us. But also… I just don't trust myself."

"Because of a mistake you made seven years ago?" Ava sounded incredulous.

Dafne nodded.

"Sis, you've grown up a *ton* since then. You've done an amazing job with Gavin, and you've turned into an awesome grownup and an excellent teacher. You're an adult, Daf. It's okay to date. To fall in love. To get married."

"I thought you wanted me to move back home."

"I do." Ava shot her a sideways look. "But you keep insisting you like it here. I'm wondering if you've really analyzed why that is, because I suspect it has something to do with that cowboy."

"No."

"A little too quick on the draw, sis."

"I mean it. I was determined from the first day." The first day. Wasn't that when she'd dumped Blake on the coffee shop floor? "I don't expect you to understand."

"Good, because I don't. You know I was holding out for Mr. Perfectly Right. And then Seth came along. He'd led a messed-up life, and he brought all that baggage — like Leo — into our relationship. But the main thing was, God had gotten a grip on him. And that made him Mr. Perfectly Right... for me."

"Yeah, yeah. Easy for you to say."

"It wasn't easy to live through, as you may recall. You were there."

Her sister was right. Ava'd had a double standard, telling Dafne that any guy would be lucky to love her and Gavin, while at the same time holding Seth's background and child against him.

Dafne sighed. It might have been easier for her sister if Leo had been part of the relationship from the beginning, but his existence had been a shock to Ava and even to Seth. And Ava was right. Blake seemed to be okay with her and Gavin being a package deal.

"Daf?"

"Hmm?"

"Have you prayed about it?"

Not unless she counted asking God to remove her infatuation and make Blake go away. "Not really."

"I suggest you start. You need to find out for sure where he stands with God, of course, but if that's a green light, why not go for it? Happiness is worth a risk or two."

Was it? Dafne wasn't so sure. It seemed the odds of being badly hurt far outweighed the chance that Blake Cavanagh could be the man she needed in her life.

"That's the ranch road up ahead." She pointed at the large sign for Rockstead Ranch.

"Wow, he lives close to town." Ava slowed the car and turned on the blinker, not that any other vehicle was in sight.

"That's an illusion. It takes half an hour or so to get up to the ranch itself."

"Big place. He must be loaded."

"It's his dad's ranch. Also, he has five brothers and three sisters." Though when Ava saw the house up there, she'd go back to thinking the family had money. They probably did, but split up that many ways wasn't going to make any of the younger generation rich.

Dafne didn't care about that. Her parents weren't wealthy, just comfortably middle class. So long as she wasn't worried where food and shelter were coming from, she didn't care much about the rest.

"It's sure pretty up here."

It was. The beauty of nature flowing by the car as they wound up the steep road should have soothed her spirit. Instead, she couldn't help wondering what the next few hours would hold. She shouldn't have let herself be coerced to go riding again. Not with Blake.

Not with her eagle-eyed sister watching.

BLAKE SHOULD HAVE THOUGHT this through. He had too many sisters, and all three of them hung around the stable as though they knew he wanted them gone. But Emma was right. The alley down the center of the stable did need cleaning, and Alexia's mare hadn't been properly groomed since last time they'd visited. They'd driven up for the day with Vivienne, who leaned on the gate to Domino's stall and chatted with Lex.

"I don't know anything about the Cavanagh history," Vivienne said. "Ms. Santoro doesn't seem to realize that this assignment is easy for some kids and brutally hard for others."

Blake's ears perked. Of course, Vivienne also was in a class or two of Dafne's. "What kind of assignment?"

Vivienne turned as though she'd forgotten he was rummaging around the stable. "Oh, I'm supposed to write a paper about when my family came to Montana."

"Eighteen-eighties. Anything else?"

She rolled her eyes. "My mom's family lived in Helena for years, but I can't ask her about it anymore."

"You could just write about what you remember," Alexia suggested. "It's not like this paper will be a major part of our grade for history class. It looked to me like Ms. Santoro thought up the project on the spur of the moment."

Blake doubted Dafne said or did anything without thinking it through. She'd probably dissected and cross-examined the ins and outs of the assignment for a week before casually springing it on her classes.

"You could ask Dad for more details." Emma moved the wheelbarrow and shoveled more manure into it.

"Not on your life." Vivienne crossed her arms over her chest as though to protect herself.

Blake could hardly blame her. It took a lot of nerve simply to show up at Rockstead since her appearance in July had caused a fracture in the family that was nowhere close to healing. No, Vivienne hadn't caused it. Her presence had merely exposed something that had already been present. It wasn't the seventeen-year-old's fault the father she'd never known had kept her existence a secret and was still being a total jerk about it.

Kathryn had acted far more compassionately toward her husband's illegitimate child than toward her husband. Again, Blake couldn't fault his stepmother.

Dad was hotheaded and stubborn, and he hadn't settled down noticeably in the two months since their family had disintegrated. Kathryn had asked for marriage counseling. Dad thought that was the dumbest thing he'd ever heard of.

What was some random person who didn't know the ins and outs of their dysfunctional family going to give for useful advice that Dad would actually follow? Yeah. Waste of time and money.

The upshot was Kathryn and the girls living in town and coming to visit occasionally, but when Kathryn came, it was to ride Laire, not to hang out with Dad.

A vehicle pulled into the ranch yard, and there were too many witnesses, but it couldn't be helped now. Blake closed his eyes and prayed for patience then pivoted and strode out of the stable.

A car with Washington plates came to a stop nearby.

"Who's that?" Vivienne asked from right over his shoulder.

Drat, the teens had followed him outside.

"Oh, Blakey has a crush on Ms. Santoro." Alexia tossed her hair back dramatically.

"Really?" Vivienne dropped her hands to her hips. "Are you kidding me? Aren't there enough women in Jewel Lake that the twins and I don't know so that you don't need to embarrass us by dating one of our teachers?"

Alexia snickered. "Oh, he's already dated all the others."

"Hey, now. It's not like that."

"Sure, it's not." Emma rolled her eyes. "Only because Ms. Santoro keeps turning you down. Though maybe that's changed?"

"Uh… I ran into her and her sister downtown this morning." He'd keep the lunch date to himself. "Her sister's visiting and wanted to know what there is to do around here."

Dafne had exited the car by now and opened the back-door for Gavin, who bounded out the second he was released. Her sister took more time to unbuckle the toddler. Long enough for Dafne's gaze to latch onto his for a few seconds longer than the girls could possibly miss.

Vivienne elbowed him as she turned back to the stable. "Seriously, Blake." Her voice was low. Thankfully. "Don't mess this up. That's my teacher, and I need good grades for college. This isn't a joke."

He caught his sister's arm. "I know. She's got a little kid. I'll be careful."

That was before Gavin launched at him, and he needed to swing the boy to the corral rail to keep him under control. "Mr. Blake!" And Gavin grabbed his hat and plunked it on his own head with a wide grin. "Do I look like a cowboy now?"

The twins elbowed each other, giggling, as Vivienne stomped into the stable.

Blake sighed. There wasn't any point in pretending to

his sisters that he wasn't smitten with Dafne... and her son. "You sure do, squirt. Want to help me with Clover?"

"Can I?"

"Sure. Your mama can bring your aunt and cousin in when they're ready. Okay?" He offered a raised eyebrow toward Dafne as he set Gavin back on the ground.

The boy grabbed Blake's hand and dragged him toward the stable door as Ava settled her toddler on her hip and came up beside Dafne.

Blake had already told Dafne how he felt about her. Seemed he might as well make a general public announcement. Maybe write a letter to the editor of the local paper or rent billboard space. Get a plane and do some skywriting.

Because it didn't look like he was going to stop being obsessed with Dafne Santoro anytime soon. And her little boy was icing on the cake.

CHAPTER FIFTEEN

Dafne had once seen a newsclip of a mudslide descending and wiping out an entire highway over in western Washington. Huge trees and house-sized boulders had been caught in the debris flow and channeled downward as though they were Tinker toys.

That's how she felt. Like she was tumbling down a mountain, pushed by unseen forces. She'd land eventually, broken and battered. She knew. She'd been there before.

Did that mean no man was a safe place, just because Connor hadn't been? And he'd only been seventeen himself. But Blake had a reputation around town. It hadn't taken a lot of eavesdropping to figure that out. Which meant he had more in common with Connor than was safe for Dafne.

Her sister might have been looking for Mr. Perfectly Right, but Dafne was looking for Mr. Safe.

And the cowboy leading a pony out of the stable with her young son in the saddle was not safe. Not in the least.

Look at how Gavin beamed over at Blake. How Blake grinned back at the boy.

Dafne's heart clenched. Could Blake be the real deal, despite his reputation? It was hard to envision, and yet... she had an excellent imagination. In this moment, she could see it.

Blake said he liked her. He obviously wasn't turned off by her having a child. Gavin flat-out adored Blake.

She was the holdout.

"Sit tight, squirt." Blake looped the reins over a post and looked over at her. "I'll be right back with the others. The girls are saddling up Laire and Lady, and I'll get Zorro."

Dafne took a deep breath. She was doing this. Allowing Gavin to ride by himself. Allowing Ava to see Blake's interactions with both of them. How could she have prevented the scenario? She couldn't. The mudslide had started way up the mountain, and now she was caught in it with nothing to do but ride it to the bottom and hope her heart stayed intact.

Click. Click.

Ava lowered her phone camera. "I'll send that to Mom. She'll want to see how happy Gavin is. She's had visions of him pining away for home."

There was no point in arguing with Ava. Besides, Dafne should have thought of snapping a few photos herself. "Text them to me, too?"

"Sure." Ava hip-checked her. "I'll get a few of you and the hot cowboy, too."

"Don't." The protest came out automatically. Not that Dafne didn't want a few reminders of this era of her life, but Mom didn't need to see them.

"You'll see." Ava winked.

Blake's three sisters came out of the stable leading the two mares. Vivienne hung back as Emma stopped beside Dafne. "Need a leg up, Ms. Santoro?"

Laire was a little taller than Lady, but she'd made it up last time okay. She took the reins from Emma, her heart thundering in her chest. "I think I can." Even if it proved to Ava that Dafne had been out to Rockstead more than once. "But my sister, Ava, has never been on a horse, so she'll need help."

Emma shot her a shy grin. "Okay."

The first time, Blake had just propelled Dafne to the saddle. He wouldn't do that for Ava, would he? For any female tenderfoot who came to the ranch? But, no.

Dafne managed to clamber aboard Laire. Gavin cheered. Vivienne, somehow holding Leo, looked at her thoughtfully. Emma and Alexia focused on coaching Ava onto Lady.

Then Blake exited the stable, leading Zorro. His twinkling gaze came straight to Dafne, and he gave her a thumbs-up before he glanced at her sister. He nodded, apparently approving of the twins' coaching, and his eyes locked on Dafne's again. "Good job."

Her heart warmed. "Thanks."

"I'm going to lead Clover. Do you want to lead your sister?" He dropped his reins to the dirt and came closer to her.

Ground-tying. The Cavanagh horses were trained to stay in one place as though they were actually secured. They wouldn't wander, even though they could.

Blake's request meant she was in charge, not only of

herself, but Ava. But she'd managed okay the other times. She gave a short nod.

He patted Laire's neck mere inches from where her hands held the reins. "You've got it, Dafne."

"Thanks." She swallowed hard and turned slightly to watch him approach her sister.

Ava was on Lady's back, grinning widely. "Oh, I'm going to love this. I've always wanted to ride, but I've never had the chance before."

Dafne had never once dreamed of riding. She'd always been terrified of the big beasts, but look at her now. She accepted Ava's reins and gave her sister a smile. "Looks good on you."

Ava snapped a photo. "Now take one of me, please. I can't wait to show Seth and the girls."

Dafne acquiesced. She took another of Gavin then couldn't help snapping one of Blake swinging effortlessly into his own saddle. Another of him reaching down for Leo — who, miracle of miracles, didn't scream at the stranger — and one more, for good measure, of him with Leo snugged in front of him.

It was incidental that Blake looked so darn good holding a toddler. It was incidental the cowboy was grinning at her while her phone camera clicked.

She was careening down the mudslide as it was. Why not see where it went?

Dafne smiled back and mouthed the word *thanks*.

Emma passed Clover's lead over to Blake, and he looked at all of them to assess. Finally, he nodded. "Let's head out then."

Where he led, she'd follow. At least for now. She could still pull out before she got hurt too badly. Right?

THE STABLE WAS quiet after Dafne and her sister had left the ranch. A quick scan showed him the twins and Viv were still out on the trail — he'd made Lex promise to ride east instead of north. And, yes, he'd promised each of them a doughnut from the Copper Carafe for their non-interference. Sue him for bribery.

Blake brushed Clover first. The pony was as placid as they came. She'd plodded along behind Zorro with nary a misstep. Every time Blake had caught Gavin's eye, the little boy's grin was so wide his cheeks were going to ache for a week.

The kid needed a cowboy hat of his own.

Blake blinked. Where had that thought come from? It wasn't his job — or even his right — to give a gift like that. But still, he could call it self-preservation, couldn't he? It would keep Gavin from snatching Blake's.

If it were anyone else teasing him that way, Blake would have snapped by now. But somehow, the little boy's glee was contagious. If Blake were forced to admit it, he didn't much mind. It proved Dafne's kid liked him. Even her sister had noticed. Ava's eyebrows had shot straight up at Blake's interchanges with her nephew.

He patted Clover, moved to the next stall, and began currying his stepmother's horse. He spent a few minutes in prayer for Kathryn and his dad's relationship. Or lack of it. Even though Kathryn had mostly kept to herself the past few years, the whole atmosphere of the ranch had dimmed when she actually moved away. It wasn't just the absence of the twins.

Kathryn had been a fixture. As a kid, Blake hadn't been all that curious about her relationship with his dad. As a teen, he'd had questions with no one to ask them of. As an adult, he'd known something was very wrong, but the problem wasn't his. Until it had become everyone's business.

Laire brushed, he moved on to Lady. And then, finally, to his patient gelding just as he heard the clatter of hoofs in the yard then the girls' chatter and laughter from the corral. At least they weren't *too* traumatized by the situation with their parents.

Emma paused at the gate to Zorro's stall, Desiree at her shoulder. She smirked at him. "You're back earlier than I thought."

"Long enough for tenderfeet, especially the little kids."

"Yeah. They're all going to have sore backsides." Emma absentmindedly stroked Desiree's nose. "Blakey?"

"Hmm?"

"Do you think my parents will get back together?"

He straightened and met her gaze. "I don't know. It doesn't look much like it at the moment, but God can do miracles, right?"

"I'm not sure. It seems more like He doesn't care."

"I can see why you'd think that. God tends to let us go our own way. It's called free will."

"So, why bother praying? Mom says we should pray for Dad, but what good does it do? It just gets my hopes up, and then they're crushed."

Blake hated that she felt that way.

"Just now when we crossed the creek behind the house, Dad was out on the deck. He saw us — I know he did — but he didn't come down or wave or even say hi. He just went into the house. We're his kids! He shouldn't treat us that way."

It might've been Vivienne's presence, but probably not. Declan had never been a particularly doting father. The boys had managed to earn occasional grunts of favor for jobs well done over the years, but the girls had fewer chores. Now that they lived in town, none at all.

"I can't explain Dad. All I can tell you is our Heavenly Father is a lot different."

"He'd have to be, or no one would want Him."

"Well, yeah. But He's a loving Father from the inside out, not just so we'll hang around."

"I suppose. It's hard to believe right now, though." Emma squinted at Blake. "And since when are you into God-talk?"

He'd like to say *always*, but it wasn't quite true. "I've never not believed."

"Maybe, but you sure haven't talked about it."

"Maybe you haven't asked?"

She rolled her eyes. "Gimme a break."

"Okay, fair enough. This whole thing with the parental units has made all of us think a little. Also, Adam and Travis, in particular, deepening their faith over the past couple of years made faith look more attractive, you know?"

"I've never not believed, either." Emma finger-combed Desiree's mane. "But lately, I'm just not sure."

Fifteen was hard, at least for guys. Apparently for girls, too. Maybe especially hard for girls whose parents' marriage was on the rocks. All the boys had been younger when Dad's first marriage had blown apart, and they'd stayed at the ranch with Dad. Mom had shown up once last summer — she and Dad had spent half an hour coloring the air blue, all blasters on high. The crew had all cleared out of the way as best they could, but the twins had witnessed some of it, too.

"I'll pray for you." The words surprised Blake, though he meant them. "Being a teen is tough. You can talk to me whenever."

Emma sighed. "Not that you get it."

"I might understand more than you think. No secret I've had doubts, Emmy. But it seems worth finding my way back to God. Making faith more personal than just something I had to endure Sunday mornings to keep others happy."

"Why did Dad make you guys go to church when he won't?"

"To get us out of his hair for an hour or two a week, I suspect. Pretty sure he wanted us to become morally decent citizens, but he didn't expect the religion bit to stick."

"Laugh's on him." Not that Emma was laughing.

Neither was Blake. He met his sister's gaze. "Your mom has taught you and Lex well, and now you're attending a Christian school. But it's still up to you guys what you do with it. It's a personal decision."

She eyed him thoughtfully. "Ms. Santoro must've been

Viv's age when her kid was born, so she's not exactly a stellar role model."

Blake's gut dropped. He hadn't thought of Dafne's age relative to his sisters. "We don't know the whole story." Maybe she'd been raped? But no, she'd mentioned Gavin's dad — Connor — by name, and it hadn't sounded like that.

He hated the guy for using young Dafne that way, but Blake had no grounds to be self-righteous about it. He'd made plenty of mistakes himself. So far as he knew, he'd never left a woman pregnant. And he'd never have pushed her for abortion if he had, unlike Connor.

Didn't mean he was any better than Gavin's dad.

No wonder Dafne tried to avoid him. But she was coming around, wasn't she? Today it felt like they'd had a moment here and there, despite her sister's presence.

How could he show her he was serious without her shying away like a spooked filly? Because, shocking as it seemed even to him, Blake was serious. For the first time in his life.

CHAPTER SIXTEEN

Dafne gathered the students' papers into her briefcase. This project was going to be interesting reading over the next few evenings. No doubt, she'd learn a lot about Montana history as well as what made her students tick.

A few history books rested on the back table. She should tuck those back on the shelf. And those chairs needed straightening, which was ridiculous, since the janitor would be through this evening.

She glanced around the classroom then picked up her briefcase and turned for the door.

Oomph.

She blinked and looked up into Blake's serious face. "Um, hi?"

"Can I take you for dinner?"

"We have a meeting with your mom about the high-school retreat." Surely, he remembered. It was going to be at her place this time, so she could tuck Gavin in bed when the time came.

"Before that. Emma can watch Gavin. She already agreed."

Oh, no. Ava had definitely noticed the sparks between Dafne and Blake. Now he was announcing it to his younger sisters, Dafne's students? That might account for the smirk on the twins' faces in class a couple of hours ago. At least they'd handed in their papers along with everyone else.

"Blake, you don't have to—"

"I want to take you out. I like you, and I want to get to know you better. Your kid is awesome, but I want to know who you are without him, too."

In some guys, that would have seemed a rejection of Gavin. A rejection of Dafne's status as a single mom. Not from Blake. Not after the many times she'd witnessed his interactions with her son.

Dafne had to take Blake's words at face value. Which meant she had to decide, here and now, whether this handsome cowboy was someone to pursue or to reject. That vision of a mudslide forcing her hand wasn't entirely true. She could decide not to be swept away.

Blake's dark eyes searched hers as he leaned against the doorframe, partially blocking her escape. If she pushed past him, he'd let her. She knew he would. But should she?

She hesitated a moment too long.

He straightened. "I thought maybe we had something worth pursuing." Disappointment laced his quiet words. "Have I been reading things that aren't there?"

There *was* an undeniable connection. Ava had made her promise to get to know him better before rejecting him completely. She'd thought she could do that little by little, maybe as they worked on the retreat plans. Not that he'd boldly jump in.

"Guess that's my answer." He gave her a rueful grin. "See you at seven for the meeting."

Dafne reached out and touched his arm as he turned away. "Okay."

Blake stilled as his gaze locked onto hers again. "Okay what? See you at seven?"

Somehow she got the words past the lump in her throat. "Dinner would be nice."

His hand covered hers on his forearm in an instant, warm and strong and reassuring. "Really?"

"Sure. Why not?" Oh, man, she knew a dozen reasons why not. Still, she smiled at him.

"If we leave in half an hour, we've got time to head into Missoula. Otherwise, it's the Chuckwagon here in Jewel Lake. Which would you prefer?"

What he was asking was if it mattered if the towns-people knew they were on a date. To protect her reputation from being sullied by his? But she'd seen no evidence he was still the guy she'd decked on her first day in town. That'd been nearly two months ago.

"The Chuckwagon sounds nice. I haven't been there yet." The log steakhouse didn't look like the sort of place a single mom took her six-year-old. It looked like a real date place.

Blake Cavanagh was asking her on a real date.

She was saying yes.

Ava was going to whoop and tell everyone in Bridgeview. But Dafne couldn't let the Santoro clan's spec-ulation run her life. At least they weren't all here, watching.

No, but the Cavanaghs were. "Are you sure Emma won't mind?"

He offered a lopsided grin. "I bribed her with cold, hard cash... and doughnuts from the Copper Carafe."

Doughnuts from the — heat shot up Dafne's cheeks. She'd grabbed a takeout coffee a time or two but never sat at a table since that fateful day. She'd avoided the doughnuts.

"Em is a sucker for doughnuts."

"Blake?" Kathryn's voice came from beyond him.

The flush on Dafne's face wasn't going away anytime soon.

He winked and turned. "Hi, Kathryn. How were classes today?"

"Good enough." The older woman's gaze flicked between the two of them as a little smile poked at her lips. "And yours, Dafne?"

"Pretty good. I've got a lot of grading to do, though. I can start on that tomorrow."

The grin widened. "See you at seven." Kathryn looked at Blake. "Am I sending Emma over, then?"

"I can pick her up shortly."

"Excellent. I'll let her know." Kathryn closed her classroom door and walked down the corridor.

When her footsteps descended the stairs at the other end, Blake turned to Dafne. "Did you drive today?"

"No, we walked. The fall leaves are so gorgeous, and the air is crisp and amazing. It helps Gavin run off a little energy before school."

"Can I give you a ride home before I go get Emma?"

She shook her head. "Not unless you have a booster seat."

"I don't." He gave her a rueful smile.

"We don't mind the walk. It will give Gavin some mama time before leaving him for the rest of the day."

"That's fair." He glanced past her. "Did you need anything else from your classroom or can I walk you over to the daycare wing now?"

"I'm ready." Dafne stepped the rest of the way into the corridor and pulled the door shut behind her.

Blake plucked the briefcase from her then twined the fingers of his other hand around hers.

She didn't have the heart to pull away. Not when she was relishing every speck of contact.

WHEN HIS STEPMOM walked out the door of Dafne's apartment a few hours later, Blake let out a long breath. They needed to recruit another male chaperone for the retreat, but he didn't want to think about that now. Not when the planning meeting had interrupted what had been a very pleasant date.

He and Dafne had sat in the Chuckwagon and lingered over dessert, talking until the clock insisted it was time to go. He'd learned so much about her family and upbringing in Spokane, so different from his own. Her dad was a house painter; all three kids had gone to college, though her brother had set aside his biology degree to start up a community-supported agriculture business with a couple of cousins. Ava, like Dafne, was a teacher.

Blake — well, he was a cowboy. Until recently, he'd thought that was the highest calling. What could be better than spending his time in the great out-of-doors, often on Zorro's back? Sure, the days were long and the work physically demanding, but it all changed with the seasons, and every day was a little different from the previous one.

It had been fully satisfying until his brothers had started the rumble about quitting last summer. If they abandoned Dad, Blake would have to do the same. And then what would he do? How could a cowboy without a job hope to date a respectable woman who had a solid career of her own? What could he offer her?

He became aware of the clatter of dishes from the kitchen at the other end of the space. Dafne, tidying up from Emma and Gavin's dinner.

How could he reclaim the atmosphere they'd had earlier? She was amazing. Practical. Focused. And had he remembered amazing? Because she was.

Blake crossed the space, and she looked up, a smile on her face.

Give him air to breathe and that smile to fortify him, and he'd stay content forever. "Hey. How did you think the meeting went?" Man, he didn't want to talk about the meeting. Not really.

"Good, I think. Your stepmom has the food under control. I guess I need to come up with more activities."

"I need to find another adult guy. I wish Nathaniel would do it, but he said they've got an event out of town that weekend."

Dafne sucked in her bottom lip. "I could ask Eli, I guess? Unless he has to preach that weekend."

Not Eli. It was no secret the youth pastor was open to finding a wife. He'd be perfect for Dafne in ways Blake could never hope to be. "I'm sure he's busy. We'll find someone. I'll talk to Ryder again." And bully his kid brother into helping out while staying away from Dafne. That should work.

"The thing is, Eli already has a rapport with the teens."

"That's true." Blake pretended to consider as he ran hot water into the sink and reached for the detergent bottle. Emma had gone all out with boxed mac and cheese. Knowing his sister, she'd made sure there was at least a carrot stick on the side.

"You don't have to do the dishes. I can do that later."

"I'm here now." Blake looked down at Dafne, standing close to his side. "You can dry and put stuff away. I don't know where it all goes."

"Okay." She picked up a tea towel.

He scrubbed a plate and handed it to her. He might not have learned this trick from his father, but it only stood to reason that helping out would boost his reputation with the woman he wanted to impress. "I really enjoyed learning more about you over dinner."

"Same." She set the dry plate in the open cupboard and reached for the next one, brushing his hand.

Oh, he liked the feel of that. *Finish the dishes first, cowboy.* "Someday I'd like to meet your brother. He sounds great." He'd already met the sister.

"He is. He's always been terrific with Gavin, even though he was already an adult and out of the house when Gav was born."

Dafne categorized everyone by how they related to her son. Check.

"He's a good kid. What's not to like?" He glanced down at her.

"He tends to scare men away from me." Her words were soft.

Blake bumped her shoulder. "The right guy won't be run off by a cute little kid."

She looked up at him.

He plucked the tea towel from her hands and dried his hands on it before setting it on the counter, holding her gaze the whole time. He cradled her slight shoulders with both hands. "Dafne, you're amazing."

"I'm really not." Dafne shook her head.

"You are. You're a great mother and human being. One I want to know better. A lot better."

She looked like a deer caught in the headlights as he slipped his hands around her back, but she didn't push away.

Blake caressed her back, letting his fingers tangle in her long hair. No prissy bun to undo today. He couldn't help grinning a little at the thought.

Dafne raised her eyebrows at him.

"I want to kiss you," he whispered.

Hesitation warred on her features, but when her hands rested on his hips, he had all the permission he needed. Her eyelids fluttered shut as he leaned closer, and he couldn't resist brushing his lips over them first. Then to her temples, her cheeks, her chin — and, when he couldn't stand it anymore, he closed in on her soft, sweet lips.

"Mama?" The little boy's voice coming from behind him

dashed cold water over Blake, not that he wanted to break off the kiss he'd barely begun.

Dafne jerked out of his arms, her gaze flicking to meet his as twin dots of red surged onto her cheeks. She stepped around Blake as he dropped his arms. "Yes, baby?"

"I can't sleep, Mama. I need a snuggle."

Man. So did Blake. He needed more than a three-second kiss. He shouldn't have wasted so much time going for it.

"Sure, baby. Mr. Blake was just going home."

A half-hour drive up the mountain to his little cabin by the creek. It would be chilly, since he hadn't been home to light a fire. The warmth of Dafne's presence was already dissipating the more steps she took away from him. "I'll finish up the dishes first."

"You don't need to, but thanks." She tossed a smile over her shoulder without quite meeting his gaze and hoisted Gavin into her arms.

The kid weighed too much for her slight build. She shouldn't carry him.

But who was Blake to tell a single mom how to care for her child?

Gavin smiled sleepily at Blake then nuzzled into his mama's shoulder with a sigh.

Blake turned back to his task. There were only a few pieces of cutlery left, which he quickly washed, dried, and put away. Then he drained the sink and gave it a wipe.

Dafne wasn't coming back anytime soon. Blake wasn't getting another kiss. Not tonight. He took his hat off the hook by the door and headed out the door to his truck.

Then he sat in front of her place for a few more minutes, grappling with his thoughts and emotions.

Emotions. Guys didn't have feelings. At least, according to Dad. But Declan Cavanagh was wrong about many things. This was only one of them.

"God? What am I doing here?" Not the *here* that meant Dafne's driveway, though it was time to start the truck and drive away. But the *here* that referred to his heart. Dafne's heart. And Gavin's.

Maybe he'd acted prematurely, even though he'd been watching for this opportunity for over a week. He'd asked. She'd stepped into his arms. She'd barely had a chance to respond when Gavin spoke.

How much had the little guy seen? How much did he understand? Blake didn't want to be responsible for messing the kid up. Instead, he wanted to be the man who stuck around.

Huh.

First time for everything.

CHAPTER SEVENTEEN

"He kissed me last night." Dafne slumped to her sofa with another glance at her son's closed bedroom door and spoke as quietly as she could into her phone.

"Whee!" Ava exclaimed. "Was it good? What do you think now?"

"It was good... I think. But Gavin came in almost right away."

A chuckle came over the airwaves. "Kids. I can't tell you how many times we've been interrupted by one of the girls or by Leo."

Dafne stroked the tassel on the throw pillow she'd pulled into her lap. "Gav had a lot of questions."

"Like what?"

"Apparently he hasn't seen much kissing. He wanted to know what it was, what we were doing."

"Oh, man. That's funny. He doesn't remember seeing Mom and Dad?"

"Mom's pretty discreet, if you recall."

"Yeah, but Dad sometimes catches her anyway."

"Whether Gavin ever noticed them or not, I can't say. All I know is his curiosity knows no bounds."

Ava chortled. "What did you tell him?"

Dafne's cheeks heated all over again at the memory. "I told him sometimes grownups who like each other kiss each other on the lips."

"So, you admit you like him." Her sister snickered.

Good to know somebody found this funny. "Well, yeah. He asked if he could kiss me. He was a perfect gentleman about it."

"And after Gavin's interruption?"

"He was a perfect gentleman about that, too. He finished doing the dishes while I tucked Gavin back in, then drove up to the ranch. I texted him a *thank you*, and we chatted a little."

"Did you see him today?"

"No. He does have to work sometimes. But he let me know there's no cell coverage by his cabin, just at the house and stable, so he might not respond immediately if he's out of range. Last night, I caught him just as he parked his truck by the corral."

"Is that an excuse, do you think?"

"Pretty sure not." It wouldn't be, would it? Why would Blake give her that line after a lovely dinner, an evening of planning the retreat with his stepmother, and the amazing moment they'd shared? Not likely.

"Was he put off by Gavin?"

Dafne shook her head, not that Ava could see. "The two of them seem to be on the same wavelength."

"So, Gavin approves of the kiss he saw?"

She tossed the throw cushion aside and paced to the window. "He doesn't really understand it, and I didn't want to go into more detail than a six-year-old needs. Aves... what if this all falls apart? Gavin will be devastated." So would she.

"I guess there's always risk."

Her heart sank. "Too much risk."

"I didn't say that. I knew about Seth having custody of his half-sisters before we started dating, much like Blake knew about Gavin. But I didn't know about Leo."

"Neither did Seth," Dafne reminded her sister.

"No. But you may recall that threw me for a loop. The thing is, you don't have that kind of shock in the mix."

Was she so certain? Blake'd had a lot of girlfriends. It wasn't completely impossible that he had a secret baby out there somewhere. What would she do?

"Daf? Don't overthink that part. What matters is now. It matters how he is with God *now*. How he is with you *now*."

"He prayed at our meeting tonight."

"See?"

"It just doesn't add up. Who he was before. Who he seems to be now."

"That's easy. It's God. Right?"

Sounded simple enough. And Dafne knew God could get ahold of people and do miracles. She'd seen a few of them. Look at her reprobate cousin Basil. The guy with no use for God. The guy with the drunk-driving conviction. And yet, he'd made things right with God after more than a dozen years of running, and the evidence was him making up with the woman no one knew he'd hurt so many years before. Basil and Hailey had been married a couple of years now. His faith definitely seemed genuine.

There were other examples, but this was one of the most pointed. Oh, and their cousin Brittany had done some running, too.

So, yes, Dafne could see the evidence of God's power in someone's life if they submitted to Him. Only, how did a person know if it was genuine in the short term? Like, before she got her heart broken?

"Daf, you say you're holding back — or should be — because of Gavin, but is that really true?"

She stared out the window down the roadway, where streetlights created little puddles of light at regular intervals. "Of course, it's true."

"Because, you know what? I sometimes wonder if you're using your son as a shield."

"Don't be ridiculous. I'm trying to protect him, not the other way around."

"Are you?"

"Of course, I am. I don't even know what you're talking about."

"I think he's become your excuse, sis. You may say you'd embrace a new relationship if you weren't worried about Gavin being hurt, but I bet you'd still hold back. To protect yourself."

Dafne turned back into the room. "Blame Connor."

"Oh, I do. But even before him, you were always the cautious one."

"Ha." Dafne forced a brittle laugh. "I don't think so. If I'd been cautious, I wouldn't have wasted five minutes on Connor Hamelin."

"You made a mistake, and now you don't trust yourself. You don't trust your own judgment. Don't trust yourself to make good decisions. But I want you to know, you make better choices than you think you do."

"Except you think I'm dumb for moving to Montana."

"Well, yeah. Besides that."

"That was kind of a big life choice, Ava." And she still wasn't sure it was the right one. It had seemed so at the time, but that was before Blake Cavanagh. He'd scrambled everything inside her until she didn't know which way was up.

"I'll tell you something about love."

She rolled her eyes. "I'm listening, oh, esteemed elder sister."

Ava laughed. "It's hard to know if you're making good choices right in the middle of it all. Sometimes it feels like you're dancing around in a blissful, romantic mist, wondering when you'll trip over something important that will cause you to face cold, hard reality and a broken heart."

"Oh, that definitely sounds blissful and romantic."

"I never promised to be the best at metaphors. But I think you get the point. Part of your brain — the only bit with any rational thought that isn't flapping around googly-eyed — keeps waiting for the other shoe to drop. Because you can't possibly deserve to be this happy."

Dafne sighed. "Because that's true?"

"No, sis. It's a lie. You *know* God's forgiven you. You *know* God gives good and perfect gifts to His children. Let Him. Trust Him."

Could she? Ava's words made sense. So did the bit about Dafne being afraid. More like terrified.

"This had better be good." Blake hung his Stetson on the antler hat rack in Adam and Riley's cabin. He hadn't been in here for a while. Who knew one of these little bunkhouses could look so homey? His sure didn't.

Travis dropped into a chair near the small wood stove. "Why? Did we make you miss a hot date tonight?"

Blake eyed his brother. "Of course." He'd meant to drive down into town, but he hadn't had a chance to check with Dafne before Adam waylaid him in the tack room.

Ryder laughed. "Don't let Blakey fool you. He's a one-woman man these days."

Adam's eyebrows shot up. "Do tell."

"Uh, pretty sure that's not why you called us together." And if Adam got on with it, maybe it wouldn't be too late to drive down the mountain. A guy could hope.

Adam and Travis traded a look. Wait. What? Since when were these ancient rivals agreed on anything? Yeah, they'd quit sniping at each other, but this exchange actually looked like kinship like that day in the stable. Would wonders never cease?

Blake settled on the sheepskin rug on the floor near Ryder and hooked his arms around his knees. All six bros were accounted for. None of their sisters, but that was no surprise. They were in town with Kathryn and were still too young to have much say.

"I ran into Jim Tenema in town today," Adam began.

"He asked what was going on up here because Declan had been by with a rental termination notice."

"Well, that's great news!" Blake looked around. Only Ryder and he were smiling. Which meant the other guys knew more. "Isn't it?"

"For March first of next year."

"That stinks." Blake grimaced. "I know you hoped for sooner, but that's better than the impasse you had before, right?"

"Riley's pregnant."

"Uh…" He scratched his neck.

"We were going to wait until we knew for sure about the house, but, well…"

Blake held up his hand. He didn't want to hear about that sort of accident.

Travis leaned forward, elbows on his knees. "What we want to know is, are you guys with us? Because we've talked about walking off the ranch if Declan didn't come through."

Blake didn't know why his older brother refused to call their father Dad. Okay, he knew. But a little respect, even if feigned, went a long way. He eyed Ryder, then Nathaniel.

Noah shrugged. "No biggie for me. I've got someone interested in buying out the farrier business, but I can hold on for a while longer. I'm hardly ever here as it is, so it's easy enough for me to say I'll stand with whatever you guys decide."

The guy was gone during the workweek over half the time and bunked out with Nathaniel when he was at Rockstead. Whatever the brothers decided wasn't going to affect Noah much.

Blake, on the other hand? A lot. If he wasn't a cowboy, who was he? It didn't even bear thinking about. His head seemed to shake of its own volition.

"What do you mean, no?" Travis's voice seemed a little sharper than necessary. So was his gaze.

Blake spread his hands wide. "And what are we supposed to do if Dad doesn't budge? You know how stubborn he gets."

"He'll give in," Travis insisted. "He won't have a choice."

"There's always a choice."

"Trav's got a point." Nathaniel looked between them. "If he has to sell a bunch of cattle or hire new riders, the community will find out, and the truth will come out even if we don't announce it. He hates to lose face more than anything."

"I'm not so sure. He lost face over Vivienne this summer. Over Kathryn moving out. But that hasn't changed anything except to make him more stubborn and more surly."

"I thought he was going to go for counseling with Kathryn," Ryder put in. "Didn't he agree?"

"He said a lot of things he hasn't followed through with." Travis nodded at Adam.

"But March first. That's not so bad." Blake didn't get the panic. "I mean, he did send the letter, right? That's progress he can't take back."

"I don't think you understand." Travis skewered him with a look.

"Pretend I'm stupid, and explain it better."

"Pretend?" Ryder mocked, wincing away.

Not far enough. Blake's elbow jabbed his kid brother in the arm.

"This affects everyone." Travis looked at each one of them. "Even you, Noah. Even you, Blake. Don't you see it?"

A quick glance at Adam's face didn't clarify anything. Blake refocused on Travis.

"He needs to know that we're not a bunch of peons he can walk all over. That he can't bestow a little favor here and there to make everything all better. We need him to commit to a solid succession plan, and it starts with Running Creek."

Running Creek had been Kathryn's ranch with her first husband, Joe. Why she'd signed it over to Dad upon their marriage, no one had been able to figure out. Yeah, there'd been something about Joe's brother trying to get his hands on Kathryn and the ranch after his death, but giving up the deed completely shouldn't have been necessary.

"Has anyone been digging into Jason Anderson's files at the insurance company to determine whether or not he actually managed to fleece anyone?"

Adam shook his head. "I haven't had time to dig into those allegations more deeply."

Too busy making a baby. Whatever.

"Me, either," Nathaniel agreed.

Too busy planning a wedding. Well, the man was *their* uncle. If they weren't going to pursue the would-be crook, it wasn't anything to Blake.

"I can take that on," Ryder said. "Branson is taking some classes on criminal investigation in law school. He might be able to give me some tips."

Blake frowned and turned to his kid brother. "You'd do that?"

"Sure, why not? It needs doing. Can't let the jerk get away with it if he crossed legal lines. Too bad Ainsley's mom isn't still alive to testify against him."

Nathaniel forced a laugh. "The things that woman hid for years, she would've been no help. Trust me."

Right. Brenda Johnson hadn't even told Ainsley who her father was. She would never have cracked, even under oath.

"Okay, thanks, Ryder." Travis nodded. "But back to the point. Will you walk off the job with Adam and me?"

Nathaniel shifted his weight. "When are we talking here? Because I have a wedding…"

"October first if the rental termination papers haven't been served for December first. It legally requires sixty days."

Ryder stumbled to his feet. "October first is next week!"

Adam nodded. "We know. It's not much notice."

"Can we talk about November first instead?" Blake rubbed his temples. A headache desperately tried to form. "We've got that high-school retreat the second weekend in October."

"Retreat?" Travis scowled. "What are you talking about?"

"Kathryn's putting it together. We need access to the trappers cabin and the trail up to it."

"I wish you would've told me."

"Why? You're not the boss of the ranch."

"Are you telling me Declan knows?"

"Kathryn said she told him."

"Great." Travis ducked his head and scrubbed his hands through his hair. "She'll have to hold it somewhere else, that's all."

"No, I don't think so."

"What's it to you?"

Blake surged to his feet. "I'm helping. Ryder and I have already bucked up enough wood for the weekend and stacked it by the cabin. It's absurd of you to make this decision with less than two weeks' notice."

"It's absurd of you not to stand with your brothers."

"Guess my opinion is different than yours." And he reached for his hat and headed out the door.

CHAPTER EIGHTEEN

H
i, Ms. Santoro?"

She looked up from her desk to see the youth pastor standing in the doorway. "Please, call me Dafne." The formal address was required by the academy, but she couldn't handle it from people older than herself... which was everyone not a student.

He grinned as he entered the room. "If you call me Eli."

"Um, sure." She stacked her papers and looked at the clock. She should head over to pick up Gavin soon. "Did you have a question?"

"Ms. Cavanagh — Kathryn — asked me if I'd consider helping out with the retreat. I thought I'd check with you before I confirmed." He leaned against the nearest student table.

Was his question supposed to make sense? "Kathryn's in charge. She knows what she's doing, so if she asked you, then that's great. I know Blake was concerned about being the only chaperone for eighteen teenage boys."

Eli chuckled. "Yeah, that's what Kathryn said. I just wanted to see if you had anyone else in mind to help out."

"Blake said none of his brothers were available. I'm new to Jewel Lake, and I don't know anyone else."

"But you've met the Cavanaghs."

"Well, yes. I work with Kathryn, after all. And Ainsley."

"Right." He looked at her speculatively. "I was wondering if you'd like to hike up Miner's Rock with me on the weekend? I... I'd like to get to know you a little. Since we work together and all."

Dafne managed to snap her mouth shut before it hung open too long. Was the youth pastor asking her for a date? He obviously didn't know she'd been dreaming of kissing Blake Cavanagh again, next time without a little boy's interruptions. Possibly, he didn't even know she had a son. "I..."

"It's okay. You can't blame a guy for trying." He gave her a wry grin. "Maybe some other time."

"Maybe." She choked the word out. The possibility was there but seemed remote. She and Blake had only gone out once, really, so there was a distinct chance they'd soon find they weren't compatible, after all. Then she could see dating a guy like Eli. Except not. She was definitely not a good candidate to marry a pastoral type, so there was no point dating one.

Footsteps in the corridor caused both of them to glance toward the door. A second later, Blake loomed there.

Dafne's heart skipped a beat at the sight of him, but his gaze slid past her with the barest flicker of reaction before settling on Eli.

Blake crossed his arms. "Pastor."

Eli pushed off the table he'd been leaning against. "Hey, Blake. Just the guy we were talking about."

That mention seemed long ago.

"Oh?" Blake lifted one eyebrow.

"I'll be joining your team for the youth retreat in a few weeks. Your mom asked me, said there was a planning meeting tonight."

"Kathryn isn't my mother."

Dafne pulled back a little at the chill in Blake's voice, even as Eli took a step backward.

"And my brother was thinking of coming."

Which brother? Dafne frowned. Hadn't Ryder said he couldn't? If Blake was insisting Kathryn wasn't his mother, was he calling her sons his brothers?

Eli held up both hands and glanced between them. "Sounds like you and Kathryn ought to talk things out and get on the same page. She seemed to think another man was needed. Kathryn's officially in charge, from what the principal said. So, I'm coming to tonight's meeting unless she gives me a call and tells me I'm not needed, after all."

The two men studied each other.

Hadn't Dad once watched an old movie where two cowboys stood at opposite ends of a dusty street in an Old West town, hands poised on their pistols, ready to draw and shoot at any instant? Because that's what this seemed like. Thankfully, minus the weapons.

Heart pounding, she rose, set her briefcase on the desk, and tucked stacks of paper inside. "We'll have Kathryn let you know, either way. Thank you for volunteering, Pastor Eli." Yep, the guy had asked her to call him Eli, but that extra shade of distance seemed wise in the moment.

"Okay, thanks." The young pastor seemed about to say more, but he pinched off his words. "Talk to you later, Dafne. Blake." He nodded at Blake as he walked toward the doorway.

Thankfully, Blake moved out of the way, but he turned to watch the other man walk away. Eli's footsteps sounded on the stairs before Blake turned back to the classroom.

Holy mackerel jealousy. That's what this had to be, and Dafne had no clue what to do about it. Wasn't this the same guy who'd dated several women at once, thinking everyone was okay with it? Worst of all, Dafne hadn't done a thing to generate his response. It wasn't like Blake had found her in Eli's arms.

She snapped the latches on her briefcase and looked over to meet his gaze. "Mind telling me what all that was about?" She measured out the words carefully.

"How long was he in here?"

"Blake."

His eyebrows rose, but if he was doing any relaxing, it wasn't apparent yet. "Simple question."

"Five minutes, tops. We were talking about the retreat. You said yourself the other day that none of your brothers was free to come, so your stepmom asked Eli. It seems a reasonable request."

"I was thinking of someone older, more experienced."

"Someone married," she ventured.

It must be hard to shrug with his arms crossed over his chest, but Blake managed.

Did she have to name the problem? Looked like it, since he wasn't doing it. "Are you jealous?"

"Me?" He blinked, as though the thought was foreign.

"Yes, you." She hesitated. "Blake, I like you, and I love how you are with Gavin. But this response"— she waved toward where Eli had been standing —"was over the top. I can see why Kathryn asked him. The teens speak well of him, and he already knows them all from class and from youth group."

"Dafne, I—"

She waited.

He removed his hat and scrubbed one hand through his hair. "I'm sorry. I thought he was, you know, coming on to you."

Dafne raised her eyebrows. "He was standing way over there. Talking about the retreat." Had Blake overheard Eli inviting her to hike? If he had, he hadn't heard Dafne agreeing. Or flirting. Or anything. She'd been tongue-tied.

"I'm sorry," he repeated. This time his eyes pleaded with hers. "I really am. I'm just so wild about you that I guess I jumped to conclusions."

Wild about her? Floodwaters threatened Dafne's balance. "I gave you no cause for that leap. None."

"I see that now. Please, Dafne? Forgive me?"

She studied him for a long moment while he twisted his cowboy hat in his hands. He looked properly penitent. "Okay."

"So, we're still on for dinner? Can I walk you down to get Gavin?"

"Sure. He's looking forward to eating at the Golden Grill. He loves their French fries." Also, he'd be a good buffer if one were needed.

"That's because their fries are amazing." Blake took her briefcase then reached for her hand.

She wrapped her fingers around his, feeling the strength and warmth. Sure, she'd forgive him, but she wouldn't forget right away. Connor was the last guy in her life to tell her what to do. She wasn't going to let anyone go there again.

Even Blake.

BLAKE'S CELL rang during dinner, and he glanced at the display. Kathryn. Which meant Eli had talked to her. Which made sense. He grimaced and met Dafne's eyes across the table. "I need to get this."

She nodded, and he could feel her gaze on the back of his head as he wended his way toward the street, his phone at his ear. "Hello?"

"Blake? I'm glad I caught you. What's this about you having covered the other male chaperone spot without letting me know? Who is it?"

Argh. He let the door ease shut behind him, glanced both ways, and crossed the street to the town park. "It's not like that."

"Then what is it like?"

Blake could hear the perplexity in his stepmom's voice. He took a deep breath. "I like Dafne."

"I know."

She did? Of course, she did. "And it sounded to me like Eli was encroaching. I... may have reacted." He'd totally reacted. Like a caveman.

"Does she know you like her? Have you talked about it?"

"She knows."

"Okay, then you might have to trust her."

Trust. That was a tough one. He'd always been sure women knew not to trust him. That had been its own protection. And then he'd followed through by making sure he didn't fall for any of them.

Until Dafne. "Trust is hard."

Kathryn laughed softly. "You think I don't know that?"

Right. She'd lost the one man who'd loved her truly, scrambled away from that man's greedy, conniving brother, and somehow landed in a loveless marriage with Blake's father. "Yeah. Sorry about my dad."

"Blake, honey, you're not your father. You have the ability to make all your own decisions. I'm not saying that how you were raised plays no role in who you are as an adult, but you're more than the sum of Declan and Monica."

He winced at his mother's name. Neither parent had been all that loving.

"I'd like to think I've had something to do with the fine man you are today. But more than that, it's Jesus, because God only knows how much I've failed you and your brothers."

Blake rubbed his jaw and glanced toward the Golden Grill, where Dafne and Gavin, thankfully, sat in a booth along the back wall. It was unlikely she could see him. "If you think Eli is the right guy for the retreat, I'll work with him. It will be fine." So long as the reverend kept away from Dafne.

"Would you please call him and tell him that? Perhaps... more graciously?"

It was a reasonable request. "I'll let him know. And Kathryn? I'm sorry."

"See you in a couple of hours, then. I love you, Blake."

"Bye." Wow. Those words. When was the last time anyone had spoken them to him? His dad? Probably never. His mom? Maybe once or twice when he was a little gaffer, not that he could remember. Kathryn? Not that he recalled. Anyone else? No.

Because Blake had done his best to keep a wall around himself, protecting himself from those who might toy with him then walk away. All bets were off if he did it first. Looking back, the patterns were clear. Had everyone else seen them but him?

Probably. Assuming they were not so wrapped up in their own lives they paid little attention to his.

He shot another glance toward the diner. A pretty awesome woman and her young son waited in there for him to return. He'd screwed up just about everything in his life thus far, but Dafne was important. He'd almost blown it with her completely an hour or two ago. He needed to get a grip on himself before he did it again, irrevocably this time.

For once, there was someone worth going all in with. If Blake wasn't going to lose out to Eli Bryson — or someone like him — he needed to play his cards right. Not flip out with hasty, jealous words.

He couldn't guarantee he wouldn't slip up again. His insecurities were bigger than he was, a big black blob impossible to wrestle. God knew he'd tried.

God. God knew.

Yes, He did. And He was big enough, strong enough to vanquish that foe in Blake's life. Blake had only to let Him.

Blake didn't exactly want to talk to Eli. Not really. He tapped to send him a text. *Hey, I'm sorry about earlier. I came off like a jerk and I'm sorry.* Should he comment on how he liked Dafne? Probably Eli had figured that part out. *Pls come to the meeting tonight at Dafne's. You'll be an asset with the teens on retreat.*

And send.

He crossed the street and was ready to pull the diner door open when a return text chimed. He glanced at his phone.

No prob man. C U then.

The rest was up to God.

CHAPTER NINETEEN

Dafne heaved a silent sigh of relief when Eli said goodnight and let himself out her townhouse door.

Kathryn had been taking notes of everything they'd decided. Now she tucked her tablet into her over-sized purse and looked between Dafne and Blake. "I think that went pretty well. You two good with what we decided?"

Blake seemed to hold his stepmother's gaze a little extra long. Whatever that was about. Dafne was just thankful the tension between the men seemed much less than in her classroom earlier. He nodded. "I can certainly manage all those logistics. I'll make up supply lists for the teens. Once I know how many kids don't have access to tents and sleeping bags, I'll figure out the rest."

Kathryn rose. "And I've got the food covered. I'll get Cook to give me a hand with prep, since I'm way out of practice cooking for a crowd."

All of which left Dafne with two major activities. That would've been easy in Spokane. They'd have gone to an escape room for one, and there were other organizations that offered activities and games. Here, she was on her own. Her online search skills would be helpful.

Kathryn tugged on a light jacket. "With Eli handling the devos and you covering the other activities, I think it will be a good weekend for everyone."

Blake didn't look in any hurry to leave. "No kids with physical difficulties? Everyone can hike in okay?"

Dafne thought through her students. Because social studies was a required subject, she'd met all the high schoolers. "Some kids don't seem all that active, but I don't think it will pose an actual problem for anyone beyond a few sore muscles. What do you think, Kathryn?"

"I agree. It will be good for them." The other teacher glanced between them. It looked like she had more to say, but she ended with, "good night."

Dafne opened the door for her. "Thanks for coming." When Kathryn stepped onto the sidewalk, Dafne turned into the room. Things had been a little awkward with Blake since the classroom earlier. Even dinner had been somewhat strange, what with him stepping out to take that call. He'd been longer than she expected — she and Gavin had been finished eating by the time he returned — and he'd spent most of the remaining time asking her son about his day.

While his interaction with Gavin endeared him to her, it almost seemed like he'd been avoiding talking to her. At least, about anything more important than how her Monte Cristo had been. Answer to that, delicious as always. The battered ham-and-cheese sandwich had become her obsession at the Golden Girls themed diner. Her mom would love that place.

Still, she could be thankful Blake hadn't made things any more awkward than he already had. He'd apologized. She'd forgiven him, so maybe there wasn't anything more to discuss. Maybe this whole weirdness would gradually go away.

Her parents were big on talking things out before saying goodnight. How about when they'd dated? She might have to ask Mom. Not on the phone, so it meant driving home for a weekend sometime soon.

Home? Where was home? Was it still in her parents' house in Bridgeview, just a couple of blocks from Nonna's?

Or was home here? This townhouse held her precious son and a few other family treasures, but everything else was thrift-store buys. Other people's rejects.

"Dafne?"

She blinked Blake back into focus. "Sorry. I guess I was lost in thought."

"You've got the hardest job."

"The hardest... why?"

He stood just a few feet away. "You know. All those activities. I'd help you, but I don't know the first thing about what teens like to do."

"As I have no idea what equipment everyone will need. But I'm fresh from both a college-and-careers group and teachers' training."

"Right. You have a lot to draw on."

Blake still wasn't meeting her gaze. Out in this rural area, he might not have had a great youth group. Eli was way too young to have been the youth pastor back then.

And, if Blake had mentioned college, she'd missed it. "I do. Plus, I'm amazing with search engines."

He managed a small grin. "My search ability on horseback is amazing. You know, looking for deer or moose or bears in the mountains. Computers aren't really my thing."

The distance between urban Spokane and rural Montana could be measured in more than miles or hours. The teens she taught were glued to their phones much like the kids back home, but she'd overheard plenty of conversations about fishing and football and gymkhanas. She'd had to look up that last word to discover information about youth-level rodeo games. There hadn't been a lot of chitchat about the latest video game. Maybe that would come in winter when kids were holed up inside more?

The gap between her and Blake stretched.

No, the differences had always been wide, and a couple of Saturdays of horseback riding with him on Rockstead land wouldn't be enough to surmount them. She was crazy to have made this big move. Crazy to find a cowboy so attractive.

Dafne pulled her focus back on Blake. No longer the cocky guy she'd first met a couple of months ago, he now looked out of his depth. Her brain latched onto something he'd said. Anything to get the conversation rolling again. "Searching for wild animals?"

"Hunting meat for the freezer."

Hunting. Shooting. Killing. Of course, she knew where meat came from. She just preferred not to think about it. She couldn't imagine doing the killing on purpose.

Blake sighed. "Don't tell me you've watched 'Bambi' a few too many times."

"You're a hunter."

"For meat. Which, I've noticed, you also like to eat."

"Guilty. But…"

"You're in ranching country, Dafne. There's a lot of wilderness around here. Half the guys you pass on the street are hunters and fishermen. We love the outdoors. We're not isolated from the realities of nature."

She wanted to bristle at that, but he was right. Nature to her in Spokane had been cycling along a paved path beside the river. She'd spotted an occasional deer or coyote. More often, a scolding squirrel. Nature had been Nonna's garden with vegetables growing in tidy raised beds. Nothing wild and untamed like the trail she'd ridden with Blake from the ranch to the cabin. "You're right that I've been raised differently. It's not my fault."

"I never said it was. But you chose to move here."

"I couldn't find a full-time job back home." Guess that proved where she thought of as home.

"Maybe with a year or two of teaching under your belt, that might change."

She met his gaze. "Maybe."

Blake shook his head. "Don't play games with me, Dafne Santoro."

"Me?" Her voice rose in incredulity. "Who said I was playing games? You're the one with a reputation for stringing women along." She crossed her arms over her chest. "I should have known."

"So should I." He strode toward the door, and she stepped aside, hugging herself. He plopped his hat onto his head, gave her a searching look, and let himself out. A moment later, his big truck rumbled then the sound faded away.

Dafne collapsed on the sofa. What had just happened?

Yesterday everything had seemed so promising. Now Blake was calling her out for being a city girl. Well, she *was* one. She couldn't help it. Moving four hours east wasn't enough to turn her into someone else. She'd met him half-way. More than halfway. Riding those horses — three times now! — had been a huge hurdle. An act of faith, really. Didn't he see that?

It was like he didn't trust her to make the entire leap. He wasn't completely wrong to wonder, but come on. It had only been two months since her move.

Since the day she'd dumped him on his tailbone on the coffee shop floor.

Was this his way to retaliate?

BLAKE WISHED he could shut off his brain as easily as he shut off his truck back at the ranch. Had he been too hasty? Too willing to push Dafne away? She was the best thing that had ever happened to him. Which meant she was too good to be true. Which meant he couldn't be the guy she needed.

Eli could.

Eli might live in a small town, but he didn't hunt or ride. He liked to kayak on the lake and take some of the teen guys fishing. Maybe a tenting overnight here and there. He wasn't full-bore mountain man like Blake.

Funny, just a few weeks ago, Blake figured he was quite

a catch, a debonair ladies' man. Wow, had he ever been kidding himself. The reality was much less flashy. Kind of embarrassing, honestly. Ugh.

He slid out of the cab and wandered into the stable. Someone had left more lights on than the usual array. He could dim those and have a heart-to-heart with Zorro. Maybe a quick ride... but that was dumb, since the crescent moon was hidden behind low clouds. He and Zorro did know all the trails near the ranch, though.

Adam and Noah sat on hay-bales down the alley and looked up when Blake came in.

Blake backed up a step. "Hey. Sorry if I'm interrupting anything."

"It's okay." Adam eyed him. "No secrets here."

There were always secrets. "Saw the lights on and was just gonna turn them off before turning in."

"Hot date?" Noah grinned, eyebrows raised.

As if. "Planning meeting for the high-school retreat."

"With that pretty teacher."

"And with your mother and the youth pastor."

"How'd you get roped into that?"

Adam chuckled. "If you were around more, you'd know Blakey's fallen hard. Must've, if he can withstand that for a committee."

"Enough," Blake growled. "Yeah, she's cute and nice enough, but I don't see a future with her."

Adam's face sobered. "What happened, bro?"

"Nothing needs to have happened. She's still an educated city girl, and I'm still just a cowpoke riding for his old man."

The guys exchanged a look. "You're not a *just anything*,

Blake," Noah said. "You may not have a college degree, but you've got plenty going for you. Also, I can't believe I have to remind *you* of that."

"I guess it's all in the eye of the beholder."

Adam shook his head. "You know better, bro. That's only true if the beholder is God."

The words punched Blake in the gut. Blake stared at his stepbrother. Was he really getting his worth from what a woman thought of him? Or, worse yet, what he thought a woman thought of him?

He was the sum of his upbringing, like Dafne was. He couldn't help being the son of his volatile parents any more than she could help having been raised in the city. But he was more than that. He'd made choices, too. They hadn't all been made for him.

Dafne had chosen to leave her Spokane home and move to small-town Jewel Lake. She'd been terrified to ride horseback, but she'd done it, not once, but three times. That woman didn't give in to her fears.

Not like Blake was guilty of doing right this very minute. He stuck his hands in his jeans pockets and looked between his brothers. "Thanks."

Noah's eyebrows shot up. "For?"

"The reminder."

Adam rose. "I get that it's tough, but you've stuck it out. It's Noah and me who've run."

"We're back, though." Noah took a deep breath. "Not so sure about standing up to Declan, but together... it just might work."

"Does your mother know your plans?" Blake couldn't

quite allow himself to align with them. It just sounded too dangerous. Too iffy.

"Not unless you told her. Sounds like you're hanging out with her more than any of the rest of us these days."

"Just because of the retreat." And the fact Kathryn had befriended Dafne. Had he messed up totally tonight? Just his luck, he probably had.

No, he wasn't giving in to that sort of negativity, but it was sure going to be a challenge to straighten out his head.

"Think we should?" Noah asked Adam.

"Maybe? I don't know. What do you think, Blake?"

Blake backed up a step and lifted both hands. "Don't ask me. She's your mother, not—"

Adam's eyebrows hiked up.

"Okay. Point taken." He needed to quit keeping a distance. The only existing barriers were ones he'd put in place to protect himself. Whoa. Was that with his parents, too? His mother had said she was moving to Jewel Lake last summer, hoping to get to know her sons. Coming in the midst of her and Dad blasting obscenities at each other, that olive branch had been hard to take seriously.

Was it up to Blake to find his mother? Or should he forget all about Monica and build every possible bridge with Kathryn?

Did it have to be either-or? Probably not.

"Gotta go," he mumbled, pivoting on his heel.

"Blake?"

He paused at Adam's voice.

"We need to know if you're in. All the way in. If we're doing this, it needs to be in the next couple of days."

That gave him through the weekend. "I'll get back to you on that really soon."

If either of them had more to say, the sharp echo of his cowboy boots on the cement floor of the alleyway covered their voices.

What was he going to do?

CHAPTER TWENTY

D afne?" Her mom all but shrieked her name.

She allowed herself to be enfolded and rocked in her mother's arms. Beside them, Dad scooped up Gavin and gave him a whisker-rub. Gavin giggled and clung to his grandfather's neck.

This had been a good idea, although possibly phoning ahead would have been better. But Mom had always said this would remain Dafne's home, and not to be a stranger. So, here they were.

"I can't believe you're really here. Say you're not going back until Sunday night."

"Mid-afternoon Sunday. I'd rather not drive late if I can help it." The passes already had a slight dusting on them tonight. Not her favorite thing. She'd rarely had to drive in snow in Spokane if she didn't want to. Transit regularly came within a few blocks.

"Let me get your things, mi tesoro."

His treasure. Dafne blinked. "Sure. There's just a

carryon and a briefcase in the trunk." She beeped the lock open. "Thanks, Daddy."

"Can you help me, little man?"

Gavin nodded as Dad lowered him to the cement steps. Then he grabbed Dad's hand and pulled him toward the car.

Mom tugged Dafne inside. "You should have phoned! But you are always welcome. You know that."

"I do know. I decided last night. That was plenty of time, but I thought it would be fun to surprise you."

"It's a lovely surprise, but it's always a good idea to let someone know when you're traveling."

That was true, but no need to worry Mom further by saying she hadn't told anyone in Montana she was leaving, either. Who would she have informed? Ainsley, but Ainsley might have told others, and Dafne didn't need anyone in Jewel Lake speculating.

She hugged her mom's shoulder. "I'm here now, safe and sound."

"Your nonna will expect an invitation to Sunday lunch."

"Yes, she will." Nonna was famous for following the family interests around, even if it meant impulsively rearranging the schedule of which son's house she'd be gracing any given week. Dafne'd thought that would lessen when her cousin Tony and his wife, Kenna, had moved in to care for Nonna, but nope. She still figured everyone else's business was her own. "It's not a problem. I want to see Nonna anyway, and I'll help you cook."

"Okay. We'll make the primavera. She likes that."

"Don't worry about Nonna." Which was like telling the

river not to flow. How Mom had endured as Marietta Santoro's daughter-in-law for thirty-five years and still managed to be intimidated by her was an amazing feat. Sure, Nonna was opinionated and felt her age gave her the right to speak her mind, but she wasn't that terrifying.

Easy for Dafne to say. She'd moved away.

The menfolk returned with the bags, and Dafne pointed her key fob toward the curb and beeped the locks. "Thanks, Dad. Thanks, baby."

Gavin managed a credible eye-roll. "I'm not a baby anymore. I'm six years old and in first grade. And I can even ride a pony all by myself."

"Isn't that danger—"

Dafne managed to squelch the rest of her mother's question with a pointed look. "He's fine, Mom. He's a good listener and B— the people where we ride make sure everyone is safe."

"If you're sure."

"I'm sure."

"Mr. Blake is nice. Right, mama? He calls me squirt."

Both parents' gazes were trained on Dafne now. Great. Looked like Ava hadn't blabbed, or there'd be a slightly stronger reaction. "Yep. Can you get ready for bed, please?"

"But I slept in the car."

"Gavin."

He heaved a sigh from his toenails on up. "Fine, mama. But you need to carry the suitcase downstairs, because I think it would run me over on the steps."

"It probably would." She smiled and reached for his hand.

"I'll take it down." Dad picked up the carryon. "You go ahead and catch up with your mother."

And, right then, Dafne's life flashed in front of her. Was she teaching Gavin the same things her cautious mother had taught her? She probably was. Moving two states over hadn't been the answer — at least, not by itself.

She tucked her arm through her mom's and gently pulled her toward the kitchen. "How did you ever let me go?" she asked lightly. "I can barely allow Gavin to go down the stairs by himself!"

"Oh, sweetness. I'll never let you go." Mom clutched Dafne's face between both hands and looked deep into her eyes.

"You know what I mean."

Mom swallowed hard and turned away to put the kettle on the stove. "It's hard. Your papa always reminds me it's our job as parents to raise you kids to make good decisions on your own. To become responsible adults capable of raising your own families the same way."

Look at the choices Dafne'd made as a teen, but she was making better ones now. "Thanks, Mom. For everything."

She'd felt the weight of her parents' expectations, partly because of her teenage rebellion. Also, because both her older siblings were married, but neither had kids. Ava had taken to Seth's baby boy as though he were her own, but that was a slightly different situation than a sixteen-year-old telling her parents she was pregnant. For goodness' sake, she'd run to a cousin she barely knew in Helena instead of calling her parents. Rob had called Peter, and Peter had told their parents then driven out to pick her up.

Yeah, she'd been chicken even then, but she'd stood up

for herself when it mattered. Come to think of it, she probably ought to pray for Connor more often. He was missing out on a lot of stuff by avoiding that he had a son, though he sent money more regularly now that he lived in Kansas and had a real job, the first one she'd ever heard about.

"So, this Mr. Blake Gavin speaks of. How old is this man?" The pleading in Mom's eyes told how much she hoped he was a grandfatherly type to both of them.

Dafne angled an ear to the basement stairs. Dad and Gavin chatted down there. She turned to her mom. "He's a few years older than me, a cowboy who works on his family's ranch."

Mom blinked hard. The kettle whistled, and she whirled around to make the tea.

"His stepmom teaches at the academy, and his brother's fiancée is one of my closest friends in Jewel Lake. Her name is Ainsley."

"I see."

Maybe she did. Maybe she didn't. Dafne took a deep breath. "I've been getting to know Blake some. We're working on a project together for the high-school students. I... I think you'd like him, Mom."

"But..."

"I know you were hoping I'd just go away for a year and miss everyone so much that I'd return and never leave Bridgeview again. And that might still happen. Blake... he had a bad childhood. His parents split up. His dad remarried, but he's a super grumpy man, and his wife left him after a lot of years. Blake sure didn't have the idyllic childhood I did."

Her mom managed a smile so quick Dafne nearly

missed it. "Thing is, he's got some baggage to deal with, and I find it more than a little shocking how important it is to me that he actually does just that."

Gavin's high-pitched giggle sounded from down in the basement.

"Oh, Dafne. My baby." Mom engulfed Dafne in a hug. "I can't bear you so far away."

"How did you manage to leave your parents in Corvallis and come to Spokane with Dad?"

"That was different."

"Was it?" Dafne held her mom's gaze. "You were twenty-three when you married Dad. Same age as me."

"Your father... he was everything to me. He still is."

"I know." She'd never doubted the strength of her parents' bond. "And I don't know if the same is true of Blake, but it might be. Like I said, there's... stuff in the way. But I know he loves the Lord and wants to do what's right. Isn't that the most important thing?"

"It is, but, oh, Dafne..." Mom dashed a tear from her cheek. "When can we meet this young man? Will you bring him home for Thanksgiving?"

Surely by then she'd know if they were going to stand a chance of overcoming the hurdles in their way. Dafne nodded. "I'll ask him and let you know. Now, are you making chamomile tea? Because I could use a good, calming cuppa after that drive."

A QUICK GLANCE around the sanctuary on Sunday morning didn't reveal Dafne or Gavin. Blake hadn't seen her for a few days. Apparently, he'd been counting on today more than he realized.

"Looking for Dafne?" Ainsley asked from behind his shoulder.

He turned to see her and Nathaniel, who held Bella. "I was. Have you seen her?" Maybe she was dropping Gavin off in Sunday school.

"Not since after school Friday. She was out the door quicker than usual and didn't stop to chat."

"Oh." That told him exactly nothing. Well, nothing except for the fact that he'd obviously blown it even more than he thought with his jealous reaction.

Nathaniel poked his chin toward the Cavanagh clan's usual section. "Join us?"

"Sure." Blake let his eyes rove the crowd one more time, but she still didn't materialize. He trailed his stepbrother down the aisle and slid in behind them. Only then did he open the bulletin to scan the order of service. He scowled. "Eli's preaching?"

"Uh, it's fourth Sunday. He usually does."

Right. Well, if Blake was going to get over this thing, he might as well face it straight-on. Wonder what the guy was going to preach on? The bulletin didn't say, which was unusual. Mrs. McDiarmid usually put that info inside.

They sang a few songs then Eli stood behind the podium. "Let's turn in our Bibles to Colossians chapter three. I'll be reading verses 23-24 in the New International Version."

Blake thumbed his Bible app on in his phone, noting Nathaniel did the same, though Ainsley paged in her leather-bound book.

"Ready? 'Whatever you do, work at it with all your heart, as working for the Lord, not for human masters, since you know that you will receive an inheritance from the Lord as a reward. It is the Lord Christ you are serving.'"

Eli paused and looked around the assembly. "Pastor Marshall has been going through a series on living a practical Christian life. There is plenty of direction in both the Old and New Testaments on the dos and don'ts. Sometimes we get bogged down in the minutiae, like where we should live, what job we should accept, and things like that."

A few people stirred in their seats. Was whom one should marry in that list, too? Eli sure would never say that out loud, not since the chairman of the church board figured Eli should marry his daughter, Stephanie, and Pastor Marshall tended to agree.

Was Eli telling Blake, ever so subtly, that God had already declared him the winner of Dafne's heart? Nah. Dafne only had eyes for Blake. At least, right now. He was set to mess that up any minute now, if he hadn't already.

Where was she, anyway? He took a quick glance behind him and around the sanctuary, but she was definitely not present. He turned his focus back to Eli.

"God didn't fill the Bible with personal directives like that, instructions that are for one person at one point in time. What we do have is a lot of general information about living a God-honoring life. If we follow those as best we can, it helps us stay in tune with what God tells us on a more personal level. So, these scriptures that Pastor Marshall has been sharing over the past few weeks are foundational to learning to follow God's will. Every believer needs to do them. Then, when you ask God to guide you in other, more specific, areas, you're already accustomed to listening to His voice. Does that make sense?"

Heads in front of Blake nodded. He shifted a little and toggled his phone off.

"So, today's principle is remembering that God is our ultimate 'boss.' We can't mouth off the man or woman in charge of our department at work then expect God to reward us."

Oh, boy. Blake cast a sidelong glance at Nathaniel only to see his stepbrother staring at the youth pastor with rapt attention. Did this mean that what the brothers were planning was a bad idea? Didn't quite line up, though. Did it?

"Doing our job with our whole heart as though God was our immediate supervisor is a great way to keep a good attitude, regardless of circumstances." Eli cracked a grin. "I don't want you to think it's terrible working with Pastor Marshall. It's not. That's not what I'm talking about at all."

Eli went on to expound further on his text, but Blake's mind had zoomed in on the situation at Rockstead. Would things look different if he lived like Eli said? As though he was rounding up cows for God instead of Dad? Making hay for God? Fixing fences for God?

One thing was for sure. Pushing Dad even harder wasn't going to mend fences between him and his sons. They might get their way — they probably would — but at what cost?

Dad wasn't a believer. What was that saying? *You are the only Bible some people will ever read.* That one. Was the gospel message obvious in Blake's life? Ouch. Not likely clear enough that Dad could see it, read it, and want it, too.

CHAPTER TWENTY-ONE

Blake looked around at his brothers gathered in Travis and Dakota's living room. "I'm sorry. I can't go along with your plan."

Adam narrowed his gaze at Blake. "The situation affects you, too, you know."

"I know."

"I thought you were in." Travis looked like a thunder-cloud about to send lightning forking in every direction. "Everyone else is. Right?"

Nathaniel and Noah glanced at each other and nodded. Ryder shrugged.

"Then—"

"Would you hear me out?"

Travis crossed his arms, and his eyes pierced holes in Blake's head. "This better be good."

Blake breathed a quick prayer. "Anyone else in church this morning?"

Nathaniel huffed. "Right beside you, bro."

"Yeah? So?" Travis's eyebrows peaked.

"Because that's where I'm coming from with this. We're all believers." Blake made a circle around the room with his finger. "Dad is not."

"Your point?"

Here went nothing. "What if we treated him with respect? I know this is a radical concept, but hear me out. What if we worked for him as though we were working for the Lord? Thought of our duties and chores as ones given by God instead of by Dad?"

Travis jerked to his feet and loomed over Blake. "What has that got to do with anything?"

"You may have been in church, but did you actually listen to Eli's sermon?"

"Of course, I did! What gives you the right to come in here all holier-than-thou and tell us we're not being Christian enough?"

"Sit down, Trav." Adam's voice was mild but brooked no argument.

Travis pivoted to face the oldest stepbrother. "Excuse me?"

"Seriously, bro. Let's talk this through."

"Blake's got a point," Noah said.

Travis growled then flung himself back into his easy chair. "Fine. Talk."

"Look, you guys know I'm no spiritual giant. None of us are. But we're trying, right? We're in the Word and we're praying and we're in church and all that, right? So, I just wanna know how us all walking off the job is going to encourage Dad to take a serious look at faith. Yeah, we can push him into a corner and probably get what we really want — equitable work and housing and clarity for the future — but at what cost?"

Travis closed his eyes and scrubbed the back of his neck.

Blake looked at the rest of his brothers. "I feel for you, Adam. I do. But is March really that far away? Nat… Trav… I know you guys are commuting in from town. Well, Nat *will* be, soon. But is that the worst thing that can happen?"

"What was that scripture again that got you riled up?" Noah asked. "Read it for us?"

"I happen to have it right here." Blake tugged his phone out of his hip pocket and pulled up his Bible app. "Colossians 3:23-24: 'Whatever you do, work at it with all your heart, as working for the Lord, not for human masters, since you know that you will receive an inheritance from the Lord as a reward. It is the Lord Christ you are serving.'"

Nathaniel plucked the phone out of Blake's hand and scrolled. "Kinda goes along with verse sixteen. I read that earlier. 'And whatever you do, whether in word or deed, do it all in the name of the Lord Jesus, giving thanks to God the Father through him.'"

Noah leaned forward, elbows on his knees. "So, that means we're supposed to do things on purpose, not just coast along the easiest path."

"That's how I read it," Blake agreed. "We make choices and tackle every situation as though we mean it."

"That's what I was trying to do." Travis scowled. "Make a choice and stick to it with intentionality."

"Big word for a cowpoke," Ryder quipped then glanced at Blake. "And a mighty big concept for a playboy."

"I'm not a playboy." The rebuttal came automatically. Once he'd prided himself in the persona. What a dumb ox he'd been.

"Yeah, we all know you've fallen for the schoolteacher who landed you on your butt."

Pretty sure this wasn't news to any of the guys. "This has nothing to do with Dafne, so you might want to leave her out of it. And also, this doesn't mean I love the way things are." Blake measured a look at Travis. "I really don't. I'd like some closure as much as any of you."

"We've got a chance to make that happen."

"At what cost?"

The words hung in the air for a long moment. Blake hated being the unpopular one. Everything in him screamed at him to say, 'just kidding,' and carry on. He was the easygoing brother. The one who could roll with anything and keep a devil-may-care smile in place. This time, there was too much at stake.

"He's got a point," Adam said at last. "Though it truly burns me to admit it."

Blake dared to breathe. He'd done little but think and pray since church this morning. Some of it for Dafne, sure, but most of it about this growing situation Dad was likely not even aware of.

He really wanted to stick it to Declan Cavanagh and watch the man squirm. Watch him eat some humble pie. They'd get that if they went ahead. They'd leave Dad with no way out but into the trap they'd set.

But they'd ruin any hope of future reconciliation. Dad might capitulate, but he'd never forgive them. And what would that do to the atmosphere at Rockstead?

"I think we need to do some praying," Nathaniel said at last.

Adam sighed. "I can probably live with letting it go. Riley's not due until May, so we'll still be into the house before the baby comes. It would sure be easier sooner, though."

"What if we all commit to praying a lot this week, and then we meet again next Sunday afternoon to make a final decision?" Noah asked.

Blake shook his head. "No can do. Next weekend is the high-school retreat. I'm going to be tied up with that Friday through Sunday."

"Two whole days with the schoolteacher... and about forty kids. Sounds romantic." Ryder smirked.

"Romance isn't the point of it. It's for the teens."

"How come the school is putting it on and not the youth group?" Travis asked.

Blake shrugged. "I guess the academy usually puts on a fall retreat. Just it never crossed our radar until this year since we didn't know a teacher or a student. We've got both barrels now with Kathryn teaching and the twins in tenth. Oh, and Vivienne." He was going to have to become accustomed to having a third sister, even though she didn't seem interested in getting to know anyone besides Alexia and Emma.

Nathaniel looked around the group. "Monday or Tuesday after the retreat?"

Noah shook his head. "That's the week I'm shoeing horses over in Saddle Springs. It'd have to be the following weekend, or you could just decide without me."

Blake was glad to note all the guys shaking their heads.

They really did need to be on the same page this time around. Who'd have thought it could ever happen? Not that long ago Travis and Adam had been at each other's throats at the drop of a hat, and Noah and Nathaniel had kept to themselves.

Here they were, mostly acting like brothers. Huh.

DAFNE ADJUSTED the unfamiliar backpack she'd borrowed from her cousin Jasmine. How was she going to carry this weight for several hours without the promise of a hot tub at the other end? What if she sprained her ankle again? What if—

Stop it, Daf. Don't be such a wuss.

The teens milled around her, chatting like magpies. A couple of kids stretched their hamstrings. She should probably do that, but she didn't really know how, and she'd look stupid acting like she did.

Across the group, Blake piled bagged tents and other gear onto a small trailer hitched to an all-terrain vehicle. Lucky guy got to drive in instead of hike.

His gaze found hers, and she looked away. For all her brave thoughts on her long drive last weekend, she still wasn't sure how to approach Blake. They'd had a couple of group meetings since, but the first time, Gavin had woken up with a tummy ache, and the second time, Kathryn had asked Blake to have a look at something on her SUV that wasn't running right.

Dafne hadn't pushed to talk. Why not? Possibly because

the guy should do the pursuing. Possibly because she wasn't completely sure she wanted to be caught.

Romance had looked exhilarating when she watched her sister fall in love a couple of years ago. Dafne wanted to be loved like Seth loved Ava. But it was easy — convenient — to forget how many obstacles they'd had to overcome to reach their happily-ever-after. And then things hadn't been all sunshine and roses after the wedding, either. They badly wanted a baby, but so far, they hadn't conceived.

Blake would make a good daddy.

Dafne was ogling him. She turned away, which didn't make the thought less true. He was patient with her little boy, and Gavin adored him. That mattered. It meant Blake accepted Dafne, warts and all. She could only do the same for him, knowing what she did of his reputation.

"Hey, Ms. Santoro."

She blinked the Cavanagh twins into focus. Behind them stood their half-sister, Vivienne. "Hi. Ready for the hike?"

"I don't see why we can't ride up to the cabin," Alexia grumbled.

Emma elbowed her. "You know why. We don't have enough horses, and it would be a huge hassle for everyone's parents to truck their horses here for a trail ride."

"That's not even an option for half the kids." Vivienne crossed her arms.

"You know Dad would buy you a horse if you told him you wanted one," Alexia said.

The older teen shrugged. "Do you like to ride, Ms. Santoro?"

Dafne wouldn't glance over at Blake. She wouldn't. "Better than I thought I would, to be honest. I was terrified."

"I don't get why." Alexia looked like she believed her own words.

"Well, *I* get it." Vivienne nodded at Dafne. "Horses are huge and powerful, and you're never completely sure what they're going to do next."

The twins exchanged a puzzled glance.

Dafne chuckled. "Exactly. But you gave all the reasons why we're hiking instead of riding." She dared a glance toward Blake as he mounted the ATV and started the engine.

He nodded toward her, just once, then headed up the trail, the loaded trailer in tow.

Just one glance, but Dafne felt it to the soles of her brand-new hiking boots.

"Okay, everyone!" Kathryn called. "I'll lead, then we'll have all the female students. Ms. Santoro will come behind them, then the male students, then Pastor Eli. If you need help, just sit down beside the trail and wait for the next adult. We all have radios to communicate as needed. Ready? Let's head out."

The girls streamed behind Kathryn, and Dafne adjusted her pack as she waited for her spot in the group.

"You good?"

She glanced at Eli. "Sure. I might even remember how to use the walkie-talkie if I need it."

He grinned. "All right, then."

Dafne fell into line, surprised to find Blake's sisters had waited for her.

Vivienne walked beside her. After a few minutes of silence, the teen turned to Dafne. "We're wondering something."

Of course, they were. "Oh?"

"What's going on with you and Blake?"

Heat shot up Dafne's cheeks. "I... it's complicated."

Alexia pivoted on the even trail and walked backward, her thumbs looped behind her backpack straps. "Why do adults always say that? Either you like each other or you don't."

Emma jabbed her twin. "Sometimes one person likes the other, but it's not mutual."

Alexia rolled her eyes. "Yeah, well, that's not the case here. Look at her red face."

"You're going to trip over a root or something," Vivienne warned.

The younger girl shrugged but turned around, not breaking stride. "Just know we're listening, because we care, too."

"I don't think Blakey knows how to settle down to one girl," Emma tossed over her shoulder.

Uh oh.

"He just didn't meet the right one until Ms. Santoro," Vivienne said. "He completely stopped dating after that."

"Is it true you dumped him on his butt like we heard?" Alexia turned halfway. "I would've paid good money to see that."

Dafne would pay good money to erase that first meeting from ever having happened. "It's true, but it was pure instinct. I didn't mean to hurt him."

Emma snickered. "You only wounded his pride."

"I still think we need a martial arts academy in Jewel Lake." Alexia managed a chop and a kick while she walked. "I know a few guys I'd like to flatten."

"Violence isn't the goal of martial arts. It's physical fitness and preparedness."

"And making sure no one messes with you."

"I guess."

"Blakey sure learned his lesson." The twins elbowed each other and giggled. "Do you think you guys will get married?"

There went the heat flush again. The only saving grace was that Blake was nowhere around to overhear. "It's way too early to make any predictions."

They lengthened their strides to catch up with the rest of the group.

Dafne let them get a little ahead, but not too far. She didn't want to be responsible for causing a gap. She glanced at Vivienne, keeping pace beside her. "I'm sure thankful your sister offered to keep Gavin this weekend."

"I hope she'll be okay with him and Bella. She's not used to managing on her own."

"I know she's very grateful for your help." Ainsley had told Dafne how much she'd relied on her sister ever since Bella had been born... and even more since their mom had passed away.

The teen nodded. "Kathryn has invited me to move in with her and Alexia and Emma after Ainsley and Nathaniel's wedding. Ainsley said I don't need to if I don't want to, that she's fine with me still living with them. Then I wouldn't have to move again until I go off to college next summer."

Whew. A change of subject Dafne could get behind. "Which do you want to do?"

"I don't know. What if Kathryn gets back together with my father before then and they move back to Rockstead? I don't think I could handle being around him all the time."

"If they reunited, I'm sure it would be because things have changed. Improved."

"One could hope. But if I do move in with them, they'd need to rent a bigger place. Where they live is only a two-bedroom, and the twins already grouse about sharing a room."

"Hmm. That's a problem."

"But then... living with newlyweds just sounds weird. You know?"

"I've got a three-bedroom. You could stay with Gavin and me."

"What? You don't even know me!"

The offer had popped out without any forethought. But it was all still true. And Vivienne *was* Blake's half-sister. But what if Dafne and Blake broke up? Things had been a little awkward lately, so it was a distinct possibility. But it wouldn't affect her relationship with her students. It couldn't.

Dafne took a deep breath. "Well, it's an option if you need one, so keep it in mind."

CHAPTER TWENTY-TWO

B lake had opened the water system from the tank above the cabin, started a fire in the cookstove, and unloaded the food coolers before the first hikers appeared, his stepmom in the lead.

"Thanks, Blake. Everything looks good." And just like that, she was in charge.

Totally fine with him.

The girls began digging through the pile of tents on the trailer, so Blake hiked across the clearing to sort that out. "Girls' tents will be over on that side. See that new outhouse in the trees? That one is yours for the weekend."

One girl wrinkled her nose, but the announcement didn't faze most of them. Kids around Jewel Lake grew up hiking and camping.

"Do you girls know how to put up your tents?"

"I don't. Dad said maybe you'd help me?"

Blake focused on the slight dark-haired girl who held a red tent bag as though it might bite. "Sure. What's your name?"

"Maddie."

"Okay, Maddie, lead the way."

He showed her how to snap the poles together and thread them through the loops on the nylon, and they got the three-man tent erected as others popped up around them. By then, his sisters had straggled in.

And Dafne, deep in conversation with Vivienne.

He wanted desperately to pull her aside. Talk to her. Kiss her. This wasn't the time, but that didn't stop the desire.

Blake recognized the two tents Alexia pulled out of the pile. She tossed one to Emma, who scowled. Uh oh. What was going on? Maybe he should check it out.

"Mr. Blake? I don't see my tent. It's a green one."

He turned to see a teen boy. "Is it camouflage? Because those are hard to spot."

The kid didn't laugh. "It's just regular green."

Blake pushed a few bags around and came up with an emerald one. "This one?"

"Yeah, thanks."

"Boys, your area is over on the other side of the clearing. There's an old outhouse back in the trees. You're not allowed on the girls' side of the camp."

"Darn," mumbled a kid.

"Josh, right?"

The boy looked surprised. "Yeah?"

"The rule is especially for you."

Blake was getting the feeling they should have had twice as many adults along. Neither he nor Eli would have any time to flirt with Dafne. He looked over to see Emma coaching Dafne on setting up the dome while Lex and Viv worked on the other one.

He scowled. Was that how they were planning to sleep? Things between the twins had been easier before Vivienne had catapulted into their life and destroyed the equilibrium. Not that it was her fault, exactly. It was all Dad's, accompanied by bad timing.

"Blake?"

He turned to Kathryn. "Yes'm?"

"Would you mind setting up mine when you have a minute? I'd like to be toward this side, close to the cabin and the kitchen. Maybe kids will think twice about trying to sneak past my tent."

He chuckled. "Maybe. Yes, I'd be happy to."

"Where are you pitching yours?"

"I'm not. I'm sleeping under the stars."

"Never understood you boys."

"I know." Blake met her gaze. "It's okay. I made a choice."

"You mean the girls took over your tent?"

"No, I mean I made a choice. There are lots of tents. In clear weather, I prefer the open sky. In rain or snow, I'll take the tent, no problem."

Kathryn shuddered. "In rain or snow, I'd take the cabin. Feel free to move indoors if you need to."

He could protest that it wouldn't be necessary, but he simply nodded. If an unseasonable storm blew up out of a clear sky, he'd do that. Him and all the students. "I'll grab your tent now."

"Hey." Eli dug through the few remaining bags. "Which one you looking for?"

Blake snagged it. "This one is Kathryn's."

Eli glanced around, but all the kids seemed occupied setting up camp. "Look, I wasn't trying to horn in the other day."

Uh… what was Blake supposed to say to that? "Guess she'll make up her own mind what she's looking for."

"Guess so." Eli socked him lightly on the arm. "Life's weird, but I guess I don't need to tell you that."

"How so?"

"I thought it would be different as adults."

Blake wasn't sure he was ready for confessions, but he slung the tent bag to his shoulder and waited.

"You know what I mean. Josh likes Maddie, but Maddie likes Rory, and Rory likes Jenna. Stephanie likes me, and I kind of like Dafne"— he held up both hands —"and so do you. Since I'm not blind, deaf, stupid, or sixteen, I've observed she likes you a whole lot more than she likes me."

There for a minute, Blake had been worried about the turn of conversation.

"So, good for you, man. Take care of her." Eli nodded at Blake and picked up a tent.

"Maybe Stephanie's worth a second look."

"Now you're sounding like Pastor Marshall. He can't see why I wouldn't sit up and beg for such a perfect woman." Eli chuckled. "Maybe she's too perfect."

Blake knew what Eli meant, though he didn't know Stephanie Simpson all that well. She worked at the bank, right? And she was just such a demure little thing who'd never dream of dropping a guy on his backside in a public place.

Not like Dafne.

He glanced over to where she crawled into the tent.

Dafne was game for anything. She stepped outside of her comfort zone even when it terrified her. Was there any chance she still felt like he'd be worth the risk? Once this retreat was over, he needed to make sure she knew what she meant to him. Because the answer to that was everything.

Well, almost everything. He'd been cruising along taking life as it hit him, but it was time to live life like he meant it. He'd started digging deeper into his faith already. Soon it would be time to pursue Dafne single-mindedly. What would it take to convince her? He'd watch this weekend and see.

"Can I help?" Dafne looked around the inside of the log cabin. It looked different with several coolers stacked on the far wall and boxes of other food items beside them. The table was covered with fixings for s'mores.

"No, thank you." Kathryn smiled at her. "The teens are rotating through chores, and I just released the last of them for now."

Right, that's how they'd planned it, only Dafne hadn't realized how at loose ends she'd feel. Blake was outside in the dusk, building up the bonfire, and Eli was likely off somewhere preparing for his devotional. She should probably go over her notes for tomorrow's scavenger hunt — no. She'd all but memorized the thing, and it was dark outside. She'd either have to waste flashlight batteries out in the tent or sit in here with the oil lanterns or out by the fire... close to Blake.

She glanced around to confirm they were alone before shifting closer to Kathryn. "Are the twins okay with Vivienne? It's probably none of my business to ask, except that I find myself bunking with Emma while the other two share a tent."

Kathryn sighed. "It's been a rough adjustment for everyone, frankly. They're all at such a vulnerable stage, trying to figure out who they are and what they want out of life. Alexia just wants to be liked, preferably by everyone, while Emma holds back a little more. And Viv doesn't quite know what to do, either. I know she's concerned about how things will change for her — again — when Nat and Ainsley get married. I don't know how to reassure any of them."

"Vivienne was mentioning some of that on the hike in."

"Oh, I'm glad she felt she could confide in you. I've worried about her. She holds a lot in."

"I'm astonished you're so kind to her." The instant the words blurted out, Dafne wished she could reel them back. "I didn't meant that the way it sounded. You're a kind woman. Of course, you're nice to her. I just can't imagine my mom being as sweet as you if another daughter of my dad's turned up."

"But from what you've said, your parents have had a solid marriage from the beginning. It's the second time around for both Declan and me. Even so, I was a little naive going into it. I knew he was divorced, but I still projected my own happy marriage over to him. Of course, the divorce was Monica's fault. Of course, he'd be different with me. I was just desperate… I don't know why I'm telling you all this."

"You don't have to, but you may. I won't blab. Blake mentioned something once about his uncle pressuring you. Something about a criminal investigation?"

"Joe's brother, Jason. Yes, he was becoming overbearing and obnoxious. In retrospect, I should have worked harder to handle him on my own and not been swayed by Declan's offers. But then I wouldn't have Alexia and Emma, and where would I be? No, it's better this way."

"I understand a little," Dafne said slowly. "I mean, I wish I'd done things differently as a teen, but then I wouldn't have Gavin, and I can't imagine my life without him."

Kathryn rested her hand on Dafne's arm. "I think your experiences are what makes you so good with the teens. I know my girls speak highly of you. When they say they want to be like you when they grow up, I'm pretty sure they're not thinking of getting pregnant any day soon. It's your sweet fairness with them all that they see."

"Oh." Dafne pressed a hand to her chest. "I wasn't fishing for compliments."

"I know. But don't think you're unappreciated at Creekside Academy, young lady." The older woman leaned closer. "Or by my middle stepson."

"What was he like as a boy?"

"He was ten when I married Declan, just a little younger than my twins. He was so lost. He needed attention, but didn't know how to ask for it in a mob of six boys. Travis hated me from the beginning. Ryder was the baby — only six — and he crawled on my lap anytime I sat down, but

Blake? He hung back, uncertain of his place in life. I think he's been unsure ever since."

Dafne nodded slowly. She could see hints of that uncertainty in him.

"Less so, now," Kathryn mused. "I think you've been good for him."

"Me? But I—"

"Yes, you. I've seen a big change in him over the past couple of months. Some of it might be from watching his father's second marriage crash and burn, seeing how our decisions affected him. But I think more of it is due to him wanting to be a better man because of you."

"But—"

"I may not have given birth to him, Dafne, but he's my son. I know him. And I see what you've done for him."

How had this become this sort of talk? It hadn't been Dafne's intention. She'd only been looking for something to do that kept her from being aware of where Blake was every single second.

This weekend was no time to act on any of her feelings. Not with nearly forty teenagers watching their every move.

Also, she couldn't completely get out of her mind the kind of man he'd been known for. Was there still even an iota of a chance he was only messing with her, adding her to his list of conquests?

It couldn't be. His mama knew him best, even if she was a step and not his biological mom.

A sound from over by the door caught her attention, and she whirled around to see Blake leaning casually on the open doorframe, watching her. The door had been closed. How long had he been listening? Had she said anything too incriminating?

Kathryn chuckled and reached for her jacket. "I'll just be outside by the fire with the teens. You kids don't stay in here too long, or I'll sic Alexia on you."

Blake shifted to let Kathryn pass, his gaze not leaving Dafne's. "Sounds like a fate worse than death itself."

"Keep it in mind." And she was gone, the door clicking shut behind her.

Dafne pressed her hands together and breathed a prayer. "I, um, we should get out there." Oh, that didn't sound definitive at all. She needed her teacher voice.

"Dafne."

The way he said her name was like a gentle touch, a caress. She swallowed hard and glanced over at him. "Yes?"

"I just need you to know something."

"What's that?"

"I've never once looked at you and thought, now there's a woman I'd like to lead on and then dump."

She blinked.

"This isn't a game to me, Dafne. *You're* not a game. Whether you believe me or not is up to you. But you're it for me. You… you own me, body, soul, and spirit."

"I think you're mixing me up with God." Her voice came out a bare whisper.

"Pretty sure I'm not. Over the past few months, I've also come to grips with how I've been treating Him. That relationship's been restored, or at least, it's on its way."

"I'm… glad."

"Can I take you out for dinner Monday night? I can get one of the girls to watch Gavin. You know it's not because I don't like the little gaffer. It's because, well, we need to talk."

"Tuesday? I'll have been away from him all weekend already. More than ever in his life."

"Tuesday's good." Blake held her gaze with his deep, dark eyes. "We're going someplace nice in Missoula, if that's okay with you."

It was more than okay. Dafne nodded.

He straightened and opened the door, a small grin on his face. "Now I can manage to stand forty teenagers for two days. Now that I know I've got you to look forward to."

Alexia's face poked around the doorframe. "What, you're getting married? How come I'm always the last to know?"

Blake cuffed the back of his sister's head lightly. "You're getting ahead of yourself, cowgirl." He winked at Dafne and stepped onto the porch, dragging Alexia out with him.

Dafne took a deep breath and pressed her hand to her chest as her mind spun. This was it... wasn't it? Was she ready?

CHAPTER TWENTY-THREE

Do you hafta go, Mama?" Gavin stood in his bedroom door, those blue eyes welling with tears.

Oh, no. Dafne'd known it was too soon for a date night after being apart all weekend. He'd been fine for Ainsley, playing with Bella and keeping her occupied. Dakota and Toby had gone over for the afternoon Saturday, and the boys had played at the park. But still.

She turned toward her son, but Blake got there first.

He crouched down in front of the boy. "Emma's gonna be here with you and tuck you in bed."

"I know, but Mama…" His gaze slid past Blake to Emma then her.

"Tell you what, squirt." Blake looked at him thoughtfully. "Can you do me a favor? It's a hard one, for a big kid."

The boy straightened. "What's that, Mr. Blake?"

Blake lifted his hat off his head and set it on Gavin's. "Can you take care of this for me?"

"Me?" The little boy's hands rose to touch the wide brim on both sides.

"Yes, you. I wouldn't trust just anyone with my hat, you know. But I think you'll take good care of it tonight. What do you think?"

"Forever and ever, Mr. Blake?"

Dafne managed to hold in her gasp. Wow, Gavin was going for the jugular.

"We'll see about that, squirt. But I just need to know, can I trust you to do this for one evening? It's special."

"Am I a cowboy now?"

"Do you want to be?"

Gavin nodded, and the hat slid down to cover his face.

Blake tipped it back in place gently. "Then, sure. You can be a cowboy."

"But Toby gots a pony."

Enough. Dafne rested her hand on her son's shoulder. "No talk of ponies tonight, buddy. Tonight's job is to take care of Mr. Blake's hat, if you think you're up for it."

"Okay." He flung himself into Dafne's arms, and she picked him up and twirled him. The hat tumbled to the floor.

Blake chuckled and picked it up. He reached for Gavin and tugged him into his own arms. "Hey, you already forgot the main thing, squirt."

"Sorry. I'll do better."

"Okay, you're Emma's now. I promise your mama will be here when you wake up in the morning. All right?"

Gavin scrunched up his face. "Okay."

Blake flew him to the teen like an airplane. "Good night, squirt."

"Good night." Gavin touched the hat on his head then blew Dafne a kiss.

She made a show of catching it on her cheek then wafted one in return. Best to get out of here quickly now, but she wasn't sure how her evening would go from here on in.

Blake held her coat then opened the door for her and ushered her into the dusk. A moment later, he opened his truck door for her before she clambered in. He stared deeply into her eyes for a moment — was he going to kiss her? — then shut the door and rounded the vehicle. Soon they were on their way out of town.

Second date. Nothing else counted, did it? Not all the committee meetings and all the stuff related to the retreat. But at least that gave her something to talk about that didn't seem quite as personal.

"Thanks for all your help on the retreat. The boys loved having you there."

"Hey, the girls enjoyed the axe-throwing competition, too." He grinned. "Vivienne was surprisingly good at it considering I'm not sure she'd ever even seen one before."

"Girls with weapons are dangerous."

"Tell me." His eyes danced as he glanced across at her.

"About that…"

He burst into laughter. "You've apologized enough times, Daf. I totally got what was coming to me."

That didn't keep her from regretting the moment. The shock in those dark eyes of his as he stared at her from the floor was permanently engraved in her memory. Forever and ever, like Gavin would say. Was there really going to be a forever with this man? Gavin might be in favor. She'd never guessed Blake would be the one to settle her son before they headed out.

"You know something?" He merged with traffic on I-90 then reached for her hand across the console.

"What's that?"

"Some of us are pretty hardheaded. By some of us, I mean me, in particular. I wasn't planning on changing my lifestyle any minute soon that day in the Copper Carafe. I was like a cow wandering along, eating a tuft of grass here and a tuft of grass there."

Dafne snickered. She couldn't help it, not once the image of a cow with Blake's face on it impressed in her mind.

"You know what I mean. I was just meandering, not taking things too seriously, not paying attention to where I was being led. Because it wasn't completely aimless, though I didn't realize it at the time."

She leaned against the seatback and turned toward him as he paused. She marveled at the sensation of his palm against hers, his hand slightly rough from the hard labor he did.

His hand reminded her of Dad's. Dad was a painter, and that was no desk job to keep a man's hands soft and manicured, either. Both men worked for a living. Sure a desk job was an honest living, too, but there was something comforting about physical strength, about not being afraid to get a scar or two.

"There's nothing like lying on the floor with a bruised tailbone to make a guy realize his life isn't going how he thought it was."

"And then she broke up with you."

He chuckled and glanced over at her. "That was my second breakup of the day."

This was news. Dafne's eyebrows hiked up.

"Felicity had just told me she'd had enough of my two-timing ways. Well, three, to be perfectly honest." He inhaled. Exhaled. "Then I came in the coffee shop to meet Marnie, thought you were her…" His fingers twined around hers.

"And we all know what happened then." She squeezed back, her thumb caressing his. "I feel compelled to apologize again."

"Don't. Dafne, you made me think. And I've spent more time in that noble pursuit over the past few months than the rest of my life put together. Even Eli and Pastor Marshall seemed to know what I needed to hear. They talked about doing life on purpose. Knowing what's needed and then doing it for the glory of God. So, all that aimlessness? It's gone. Thanks to you."

"Thanks to God, you mean."

"He used you."

"He's used you in my life, too."

"Oh?" Blake quirked an eyebrow in her direction.

"You might have been aimless, but I was afraid to let go and trust anyone."

"You were terrified of riding."

"Of living. Of making mistakes. Of ruining Gavin's life. Of so many things."

"And yet you're the bravest person I know."

She shook her head with a little scoff. "You can't mean that."

"But I do. Bravery isn't the absence of fear, you know.

It's facing your fear and doing stuff anyway. You did that by pursuing a job in Jewel Lake and moving so far from home." His fingers slid along hers, igniting warmth anew. "By getting on that horse despite your dread. Not once, but three times. Maybe you'll do it again sometime soon."

There'd been something exhilarating about sitting atop such a large, gentle beast. "I'd like that." She even meant it.

"So would I." He held her gaze for several seconds before turning back to the road.

THEY'D HAD A LOVELY steak dinner to soft music and candlelight, but Dafne'd picked at her plate. Blake hadn't eaten all that heartily himself. It seemed just breathing and looking at Dafne across the small table was like sustenance to him.

Huh. That was unbelievably sappy. His brothers would mock him mercilessly for the thought. Maybe not Nathaniel, who was Mr. Sensitive. Maybe not Travis or Adam, either. Weren't those guys crazy in love with their wives?

Blake was crazy in love with Dafne. The assurance settled on his shoulders like the perfectly fitted tux he'd worn to Travis and Dakota's wedding. Nah, more how his favorite Ariat boots cushioned his feet even after a long day in the saddle. Or how his Stetson molded to his head.

He knew what he was getting young Gavin for Christmas: a cowboy hat of his own. Boots. Maybe a pony, depending on how things went with Dafne in the next couple of months. Yeah. He liked the idea. Liked all of it.

Across the table, her blue eyes shone in the candlelight as she looked at him. No one had ever looked at him like he was amazing before. Never. It felt strange. Undeserved. But maybe the expression was reciprocated in the way he gazed at her.

"Are you sure you don't want dessert?"

She shook her head. "I'm sure it would be delicious, but I couldn't eat another bite." She set her fork down, as though she was finally done pushing those last few bites around. Her nervous actions made Blake think of a restless pup rounding up stray cattle.

"Let's go then." The waiter had brought the check a while back. Blake would catch it on the way out the door. He rounded the table and pulled her chair back as she rose. He helped her into her coat, his hands tingling as he settled it across her shoulders.

A few minutes later they stepped out into a star-studded night. "Want to go for a walk along the river? It's just across there." He slid one arm around her waist and leaned closer as he pointed.

"Sure. That sounds nice." Was her voice breathless, or was that just him? Maybe both.

How long did a guy need to wait before he proposed? Longer than this. He knew it, but now that he was doing things with purpose, he didn't want to waste another month or week or even day. But there was purpose and then there was panic. And Dafne was worth the wait.

They crossed the street, and she slipped her arm around him, too, as they strolled into the park.

"I told my parents about you when I was home," she said at last.

"Oh? Your sister hadn't spilled the beans?"

"Not... everything. Because she didn't know everything."

His heart hammered. "What kind of everything are we talking about here?"

"The kind where you mean a lot to me."

Blake turned toward her under the lamplight and captured both her hands in his. "I love you, Dafne. That's the kind of *a lot* you mean to me."

She ducked her face, and he held his breath for a moment before gently lifting her chin.

"Might you feel the same about me?"

"I might," she murmured. "I do. I love you."

He whispered his lips across hers, desperate for more, yet reveling in the spark of the gentle contact. "Dafne."

She let go of his hands and wrapped her arms around his neck.

Blake held her close, ready to go in for another kiss, a real one this time, one where he could tell her without words how very very much she meant to him.

Dafne leaned back a little, looking into his eyes without her guarded mask getting in the way. "Kiss me?"

"There's nothing I'd like more." Almost nothing. His hands roved her back, as he poured all his feelings out of his eyes as he inched closer.

"How about right now?" Both hands on his collar, she slowly drew his face toward hers.

"Now's good," he whispered against her lips. "Now's really, really good." And then he covered her mouth with his.

She tasted of everything pure and good and lovely. She tasted like his future.

CHAPTER TWENTY-FOUR

Blake shifted in his saddle to check on the two packhorses trailing behind Zorro while carrying a six-point elk. Lots of good eating there, and his mind drifted to Dafne, as it nearly always did. He'd cook her a steak dinner in the cabin. Her and Gavin. Nothing like a six-year-old chaperone to make sure he kept in line.

"Blake?"

He scanned the back trail, but Noah's voice came from further back. Hadn't his stepbrother been right behind the packhorses just minutes ago? "Yo! Where are you?"

"Didn't you see the pups?"

"Pups?" Blake laughed. "Why would there be dogs up here? We're still twenty minutes out from the ranch."

"The road out from town loops not far from here. And however they got here, there's four of them. C'mere."

Blake shook his head. The packhorses weren't trained to ground-tie like their riding mounts were. "Seriously, Noah? Can't we come back after we get the elk offloaded and in the cooler?"

"It'll just take a minute. Or never mind — I'll catch up in a bit."

His rolled eyes were a waste since his brother couldn't see them, but whatever. Blake swung off Zorro's back and dropped the reins. The other two wouldn't likely wander since they were clipped to Zorro with leads. Blake stomped back up the trail.

Sequoia seemed as interested as Noah in the wiggling mound of golden puppies beside the trail.

How on earth had Blake not seen them? Maybe they'd tumbled closer after he'd passed by. But they didn't look up for feats of gymnastics. They looked small. Weak. He scowled. "Who'd just dump a litter of puppies?"

"No clue, but it should be a criminal offense. Help me load them into my pack."

"Uh... Noah... we don't need four more dogs at the ranch."

Noah looked up from his crouch and glared at Blake. "What do you propose we do, just leave them here for the wolves? I think not. We can get them recovering, get their shots, try to find them homes."

The bleeding-heart brother. Not that Blake wanted them attacked by wolves or coyotes or mountain lions, all of which prowled the backcountry. All of them hungry as Montana tipped toward winter. Snow had already descended halfway down the mountains north of the ranch. But those scrawny little things couldn't be more than three or four weeks old. They needed their mama, still.

Blake prowled around in the bush for a few minutes but didn't come up with any clues or, thankfully, any more puppies. He turned back to see Noah settling a barely squirming pup into his backpack.

Sheesh, a guy couldn't stack four dogs and expect the bottom one to breathe. "Here, let me get my pack. I'll take two of them."

"Thanks, bro." Noah flashed him a grin. "I'll take care of them when we get home."

"Right. You're on the road five days a week, four weeks out of six."

"I know. But I've got a couple of days now." Noah lifted one close to his face. "Hey, little fella. Everything will be all right. You'll see. Just hang in there."

Blake couldn't help the laugh that rang out. "Dude, do you even hear yourself? And you wonder why you haven't found a woman yet. Poor girl will never know when you'll come home with a stray."

Noah lifted the pack to his shoulders and shrugged it into place. "Adam and Riley might like one of these over at Running Creek."

"They're not moving until spring." Hadn't they all agreed not to push Dad into a corner? Though some of them had conceded more willingly than others.

"God can work miracles."

"For Adam and Ry or for the pups?" Blake settled his own loaded pack in place. Good thing he and Noah had eaten all their food, or he wouldn't have had room in there.

"Any of the above."

Noah might have more faith in God than the rest of the brothers combined. But it wasn't a competition. Blake had grown a heap in the past few months, too. Was that all thanks to Dafne, or had he been on this journey before that?

Back in the saddle — with a slightly heavier load — Blake angled back to look at Noah. "Is it too soon for me to propose?"

Noah blinked at him in surprise. "You're asking me? How should I know? I'm not the cowboy with experience here."

"Yeah, well, you're the cowboy who's actually present."

"I don't know. Have you prayed about it? Plus, she's got a kid. What would Gavin's response be? And one more thing — is it too old-fashioned to ask her dad?"

All that told Blake his brain was jumping the gun. "I haven't even met her parents. Just her sister and nephew."

Noah chuckled. "Well, she's met our motley crew. Seen Declan at his worst and my mom at her best. Hasn't scared her off yet, huh?"

"Not yet." Blake drummed his fingers on his leg. "Do you think I should make an effort to get to know my own mother?"

"No clue. That's totally between you and God."

"Wow, you're sure big on passing the buck today."

"Pointing you at your Heavenly Father isn't precisely passing the buck."

"True. Well, you're right. It's not something I've given much thought to, and even less prayer. I really don't want her in my life. Everything's too messed up as it is, and she's like a lit match while the tension around Rockstead is pretty much a keg of gunpowder. Inviting her into the mix would blow the whole thing off its axis."

"God knows. Ask Him."

Blake grunted. The trail widened as they rounded the last curve to the homeplace, and Noah nudged Sequoia up beside Zorro.

A battered gray pickup sat beside the corral, and a heavyset man stood beside it, talking to Dad.

"Who's that?" Blake asked his brother in a low voice.

"Not sure — looks like Jim Tenema?"

"The Running Creek renter? What's he doing here?" Not that Noah knew the answer any more than Blake did. Blake pressed his heels to Zorro's sides before remembering the packhorses. He growled as the man opened his truck door as though he might be leaving.

Noah shot him a look. "I'll go." He clicked to Sequoia and cantered toward the scene.

What on earth was going on? Man, Blake hated having to wait to find out.

"HEY." Dafne stretched a little to kiss the cowboy at the door then pulled him into the living room. She could get used to this.

"Mama. You kissed Mr. Blake."

Oops. A quick glance behind her revealed Gavin standing in his bedroom door. He'd put on his pajamas, just like she'd asked. Only, he wasn't usually this fast.

Blake squatted just inside the door. "Hey, squirt. Wanna wear my hat for a few minutes?"

Gavin shot Dafne a glare that said this conversation wasn't over, but he dashed across the space and allowed

Blake to set the brown felt hat in place. "Do I look like a cowboy now?"

"You sure do, squirt." Blake rose, the boy in his arms. "So, you saw me kiss your mama. What do you think of that?"

Her son angled his head so far to the side Dafne wondered if the hat was going to hit the tile floor. "Why did you kiss her?"

"Because I like her a lot." Blake's gaze met Dafne's over Gavin's shoulder.

Was he asking for help? Because she wasn't giving it. She crossed her arms and raised her eyebrows, but she couldn't quite stop the smirk from spreading.

"Mama told me not to kiss the girls at school, that I was too young to like them. She said kissing is special."

Blake chuckled in response. "She's right. Kissing is special. Very special. Can I tell you a secret?"

Gavin glanced toward Dafne and lowered his voice. "Mama can prolly hear you."

"She probably already knows this secret, but not everyone does."

"Okay…" Gavin leaned in and the hat knocked into Blake's nose. "Sorry."

Dafne barely dared breathe. Blake wouldn't… would he?

"I love your mama, squirt. And I love you, too. It's more than liking."

"Does that mean you're going to be my dad? Because I already have a dad. I think. Right, Mama?"

Dafne stepped closer and felt the security of Blake's free arm slide around her waist. "You do have a dad, but he lives very far away." She took a deep breath. "And he doesn't love us. Not like Mr. Blake does."

"Is it okay to have two dads?"

She rubbed her little boy's back. "It's okay. Uncle Al went to heaven, but Uncle Charlie is Michael's new daddy." Not that Gavin remembered when his great-uncle had passed away.

"Did my dad go to heaven, too?"

Dafne tugged Gavin into her own arms. The hat tumbled to the floor, and Blake set it on the hook while Dafne carried her little boy to the sofa and settled there with him. "No, baby. Your dad isn't in heaven." She really needed to pray more for Connor, though. She didn't want him back in her life — never had, really — but wouldn't it be amazing for him to find faith in Jesus? She'd be thrilled for him.

Blake nestled beside her, slid his arm around her, and tucked his finger under Gavin's chin.

She held her breath. It was too early for this sort of talk, wasn't it? Gavin was pushing Blake's hand. Pushing their relationship with his questions. What if Blake didn't really want to settle down?

"I think kids need a mom and a dad who love each other and want to be together."

"And then there's a wedding? Like Auntie Ava and Uncle Seth?"

Dafne didn't dare glance at Blake, but she could hear the soft intake of his breath as she clutched Gavin tighter than he wanted to be held. Her son pushed away a little.

"Your mama and I haven't really talked about weddings,

squirt. But that's part of the secret, okay? That maybe there'll be one of those."

"Maybe?" Gavin shoved out of Dafne's arms and jumped to the floor. He looked between them with a scowl. "When Mama says that, it usually means no."

Ouch. Guilty.

Blake's hand cupped Dafne's shoulder and rubbed it gently. "This time it means almost-for-sure yes. But there are still things your mama and I need to talk about before we decide for certain. Can you be patient?"

The little boy plopped his fists on his hips. "I'm gonna ask Santa for a cowboy daddy for Christmas."

"Gavin!" Talk about mortification.

Blake laughed. "You go ahead, but you know who's really in charge? It's God. So, it's more important you ask Him in your prayers. That's what your mama and I are doing."

"Will you read me a story and say my bedtime prayers with me?"

"I sure will." Blake kissed Dafne's temple then rose to his feet, tugging her up with him. "You go pick a story, squirt, and I'll be right there."

Gavin looked between them as though he wasn't sure if Blake could be trusted.

Once again, Blake squatted at her son's level. "I promise. And when I promise something, I'll do it. Okay?"

"Okay." Gavin dashed for his bedroom.

Dafne took Blake's hands and helped him rise, not that he couldn't do it without her. Wasn't that just like life? She'd managed okay without him for twenty-three years, but *with* him? It would be so much better. Her heart pounded as she looked up into his dark eyes.

Blake's fingers lightly brushed her cheek. "I love you, Dafne. I didn't say anything to Gavin that I wasn't planning on saying to you sometime soon."

"I've been meaning to ask you…"

"Yes?" He swept his lips over hers, setting them on fire.

"My parents want me to bring you home for Thanksgiving weekend. Can you — is that something you'd like to do?"

His smile was so big it crinkled the corners of his eyes. "I would absolutely like to do that. But right now, I've got a date with a six-year-old. Be back in a few."

She touched her lips to remember the sweet kiss as he strode toward Gavin's room. A minute later, she could hear his even voice reading to Gavin.

Could she really be this lucky? But it wasn't luck. Blake was a blessing dropped from heaven above into her life, just when she'd thought she'd be raising her son all the way to adulthood alone. She'd been prepared to do it, too. She hated asking anyone for help — always had.

But Blake? He was worth giving up control for.

Dafne turned for the kitchen and put on water for tea. She'd baked Aunt Winnie's pumpkin cranberry muffins yesterday, and couldn't wait to share a few with Blake.

She couldn't wait for him to meet her entire extended family. Poor Blake had no clue what he was in for, but somehow, he'd manage.

There was a man who always landed on his feet. Except for that one time when it seemed he hadn't… but really had.

CHAPTER TWENTY-FIVE

W e've heard so much about you." Mrs. Santoro held the door open, but her smile didn't look too enthusiastic.

Dafne's dad swung Gavin to one hip and shook Blake's hand firmly, staring straight into his eyes. All assessment, without a hint of a smile.

Uh oh. Blake had his work cut out for him with Dafne's parents. Maybe if he had a daughter and a grandson he'd be leery of the cowboy who snatched them away, too. With any luck, he'd get a chance to test that theory someday. Dafne was such an amazing mother to Gavin. Wouldn't she want to give her son siblings?

Blake managed to smile as he pulled his hand away from Dino's grip. "It's nice to meet you both."

Dafne's fingers twined around his. "It's good to be home. Are Ava or Peter here?" She nudged the door shut behind them.

"Not tonight. They'll be here tomorrow, and Sadie's dad, Eliza, and the girls are coming for turkey dinner."

Dafne had told him all about her siblings and their spouses' families, so he had a clue who those people were. Blake might have more siblings — it took a lot to trump the Cavanagh crew — but the scope of the Santoro extended family made his brain seize.

"How about Nonna?" Dafne asked. "I want her to meet Blake, too."

Dino nodded at his daughter. "She heard, so she'll be here for dinner tomorrow."

"Oh, good!"

"Let me take your coats." Betta opened the nearby closet. "And then we'll have some decaf and biscotti. I'm sure Gavin needs a snack before bedtime."

"I do, Nonna! I'm so very hungry."

His plaintive words seemed to break the ice as everyone laughed. Blake helped Dafne with her jacket. "I should bring in our bags before getting too comfortable."

"I'll give you a hand." Dino shoved his feet into unlaced boots.

The two of them carried the three bags back into the house with no words between them. Was Dafne's dad always this quiet, or was it because of Blake? It was going to be traumatic to manage to ask this man to bless Blake's relationship with his daughter. Blake shoved the thought aside. Either way, tonight wasn't the time. It was late Wednesday evening, and they weren't returning to Jewel Lake until Sunday afternoon. There was plenty of time.

"Guess what, Nonna!" Gavin's voice came from the kitchen beyond. "Mr. Blake's got a puppy! She's very soft except sometimes she bites me."

Blake chuckled as he toed off his boots.

"Puppies do that," came Betta's voice. "What's her name?"

"It's Salem. Mr. Blake says that means peace, but I don't think she understands that part, because all the puppies roll around and bite each other. That's not peace, is it, Nonna?"

"We're putting you in Peter's old room, just down the hallway here," Dino said. "Dafne and Gavin took over the basement area a few years ago."

Blake didn't need the warning, but he heard it loud and clear. "Thank you. That sounds perfect." As his host pushed open the door to a space decorated like a basketball locker room, he noted it was right across from the master bedroom. But then, the entire house was much smaller than the mansion at Rockstead where he'd grown up. He'd like something in between for him and Dafne and Gavin, but closer to this. Small enough to be homey. He set down his own roller case and followed Dino back to the kitchen.

"Mr. Blake said—" Gavin's voice cut off when he spotted Blake entering the kitchen. He slid off the tall stool by the counter and darted over.

Blake lifted him. "Hey, squirt. What did I say?"

Gavin nestled his head into Blake's neck. "Will you read me my bedtime story?"

"Sure will. Did you pack the chapter book?" He'd been reading 'The Indian in the Cupboard,' a favorite from his own childhood, aloud to Gavin several evenings a week.

"I did! Right, Mama?"

"He sure did. It's right on top of his duffel bag."

Blake cast a glance at Dafne as he rubbed Gavin's back. "Is it bedtime now?"

Gavin leaned against Blake's face. "I want my story."

"Sure. I'll just get our luggage if you want to carry him down." Dafne pointed to the open staircase off the dining area.

"Let me."

She rolled her eyes. "You can't carry him and two bags."

"I'll get the bags." Dino gave his daughter a side-hug. "You just visit with your mama, mi tesoro."

Whatever that meant, it sounded like a sweet nickname. "Okay."

Blake followed the man down the stairs to a walk-out basement with a small living area and two tiny bedrooms. This would have been every teen's dream come true, but it likely hadn't been Dafne's. Not when she'd chosen to raise her son with her parents' help while she finished school. She'd made so many sacrifices.

He set Gavin down and the boy dashed into the bathroom. Splashing sounds revealed he'd washed up before he erupted back out. Dino lifted Gavin's bag onto the twin bed in another basketball-themed room. Was that Gavin's preference? Because Blake had been envisioning cowboys like his own nephew's room. Toby was obsessed with Woody from Toy Story as well as *real* cowboys.

Blake only dared to glance into Dafne's room because her father's back was turned, and his eyebrows shot up. Pink, purple, and giant flowers. That didn't seem like her at all. Of course, her place in Jewel Lake was construction beige like most rentals he'd seen.

What would she really like? Where would they live? As Gavin changed into his pajamas and chattered at his quiet grandfather, Blake remembered the glee on Adams' and Riley's faces when they'd found out that Jim Tenema was leaving Running Creek at the end of November, three months before the original termination. Right when Adam originally asked for, but Jim didn't know that. He was only moving earlier because he'd landed a new job in Seeley Lake.

Everyone was happy, especially Riley, and no one had needed to push Dad's buttons. So, at least one Cavanagh brother would soon have the home he wanted for his growing family. The brothers still planned to meet with Dad soon about Travis's and Nathaniel's situations. About the whole transition to give some security to the next generation. They'd talked about doing this over Thanksgiving weekend until Blake had said he was going to Spokane with Dafne. There'd be time. After all, Travis wanted to build, and Nathaniel thought that was a great idea, too, but it wasn't like construction could start at this time of year.

Gavin came running out, carrying the paperback. He grabbed Blake's hand and towed him to the small sofa. "Read to me, Mr. Blake."

"Sure thing, squirt." Blake tucked the little boy tight against his side and opened the book where an envelope marked their spot.

"Come upstairs and kiss your nonna goodnight when you're done," Dino said as he headed to the stairs.

"I will, Nonni. And Mama wants me to brush my teeth, too. I remember."

The look Dino Santoro leveled at Blake as he left the space was a mix of regret and approval.

Blake thought that maybe, just maybe, he understood that dichotomy completely.

"THAT WAS QUITE THE GAUNTLET." Blake merged his pickup onto I-90 on Sunday after dinner and grinned over at Dafne.

"I'm sorry." She'd known it would be a lot for him to take in.

"Don't be."

She glanced back at Gavin, who had his headphones on as he played a game on her tablet. Then she placed her hand, palm up, on the console between her and Blake.

His palm felt warm and safe against hers even though he didn't grasp tightly. That was okay — he might need to pull away suddenly, depending on traffic. She reveled in the sensation of his skin against hers in a way she'd never considered before this man.

"So… have I met everyone?"

"Not quite, believe it or not. A few of my cousins didn't make it back for Thanksgiving. I really need to make the effort to get over to Helena one weekend to see Rob and Bren. It's not that far from Jewel Lake, but things have been busy."

"I can take you sometime. In fact, there's a big concert there in December. Christmas at the Cathedral, I think it's called. Why don't I see if I can get us tickets?"

"Oh, that sounds amazing." See? This was one more reason to love this man. He was so thoughtful.

"Your dad is really protective of you."

Dafne couldn't help the smile. "I know. I'm his baby, and he feels like he failed me once already."

"I'd probably feel the same way if I had a daughter." His thumb slid across her knuckles.

Who knew a hand contained so many nerve endings? Or that so much meaning could be layered into such a short comment? Ava had dragged her shopping on Black Friday, but Blake had opted to stay back at the house with Gavin. Had he and Dad had a talk?

Because that would mean… but, no. She and Blake had only known each other four months and been dating for half that. It was much too soon for any declarations.

It didn't feel too soon, though. Her heart was at home, safe in his hands in a way she'd never believed could happen.

"Your dad told me that the mushy feeling we call love doesn't last. I'm not sure I believe him." Blake shot a glance her way again.

Well, that was a change of subject. "My parents have said that before. I remember overhearing them talking to my sister-in-law about that once, when she and Peter were dating."

"It kind of scares me. I'm sure my father and Kathryn were once in love, but it's hard to remember."

Dafne angled in the seat to better view Blake's profile. "Didn't my dad explain what he meant?"

"He did, but I was wondering what you thought of it."

She pursed her lips. "He means that we — the population in general — tend to think of love equaling the giddy feelings, the rapid heartbeat, and all that. But that's just chemistry—"

"I like chemistry more now than I did in high school."

"Me, too." She laughed. "But love is deeper than that. Dad told me..."

Blake's fingers clasped hers tightly. "That love is a choice. It's an action. Something we do on purpose, not because we feel all lovey-dovey."

"Yeah."

"I'd never thought of it that way before. Maybe that's why Kathryn stayed for so long. Because she'd chosen to love Dad even when he was unlovable. Long after the heart palpitations wore off."

A glance into the backseat revealed Gavin nodding off with his headphones still in place. "Palpitations?" she asked softly. "You've got some of those?"

"Oh, baby, you have no idea."

The intensity in his low voice sent a shiver through her. A good shiver.

"I just want you to know I understand love a little better than I did. And why it sometimes seems to disappear, while other times it stays and grows."

He must be thinking of his brothers as well as his dad. "I think mutual faith makes a big difference. Although I've known too many Christian couples who've grown apart and split up."

Blake looked her direction then back at the highway. "Could some of those marriages have been saved?"

"Some could, I'm sure, but maybe not all. You're right, though — or Dad is — that love is a verb, an action word. Sometimes we have to act in faith, and then what we are looking toward gains a foundation and becomes real."

"Not magically."

She shook her head. "No. It's not like wishing on pixie dust, but believing God has a plan for our lives, then stepping out in faith to do our part."

"I spent too many years drifting along like a will o' the wisp. Meeting you... well, it made me see what I was doing. You've given my life meaning."

"Only God can do that."

His fingers caressed hers. "Being kicked to one's backside on a cement floor can — shall we say — make a big impression, too." He flashed her a grin.

Dafne's face flushed. She was never going to live down their first meeting, but maybe that was okay. He'd earned it. But the things he deserved now? She'd kiss him if he weren't driving.

"Just want you to know, I'll love you like I mean it every day God gives me to do it."

His voice was so low she almost missed that promise. It wasn't a proposal, but hadn't she decided it was too early for that, anyway? It definitely gave her assurance the day was coming.

She could wait. And she could love him back the very same way.

CHAPTER TWENTY-SIX

Dafne could hardly breathe for the beauty of the Creekside Fellowship sanctuary. Ainsley had chosen red, black, and white for her wedding colors, and they'd massed the platform with poinsettias. Bits of winter greenery with red velvet bows adorned the ends of the pews. The whole effect was mesmerizing in the flickering candlelight.

She glanced up at the handsome cowboy who held her hand. No flannel shirt, jeans, or cowboy hat today — the man cleaned up nicely in a black tuxedo with a white carnation on his lapel. The shiny black footwear below his trouser legs did happen to be cowboy boots, though. She couldn't hide the grin — she wouldn't have expected anything else.

"What's so funny?"

"Nothing," she murmured. "You look great."

"Not a fraction as amazing as you look, Ms. Santoro. That blue brings out the color of your eyes."

It had been difficult to decide what to wear to Ainsley

and Nathaniel's wedding. Dafne had a sweet little red dress, but that seemed presumptuous with the bridesmaids in crimson. And, while black might be formal and always suitable, she didn't love the look on her. Sapphire blue, though? It did bring out her eyes, and she thrilled at the knowledge Blake had noticed.

Dafne loved that she recognized so many of the people present for this winter wedding. She smiled at Ms. Cantrell, the academy principal, and Stephanie Simpson, the bank teller. Pastor Marshall and Pastor Eli were sharing the officiation, while Ellen Jones bent over the grand piano, the no-doubt-beautiful notes barely audible over the low murmur of guests waiting to be seated.

Adam and Noah did the ushering honors, and soon Dafne and Blake were next in line. Adam extended his elbow to Dafne with a wink, and she took it.

"How are you guys settling into your new place?" she asked quietly as he guided her down the aisle.

"Great! You two will have to come out for New Year's Eve, if you don't have other plans. Bring Gavin. We have lots of room."

"We'll talk about it. Thanks for the invitation."

Adam gestured her into a row just behind where Emma and Alexia sat with Ryder between them.

"Thanks, man," she heard Blake say to Adam as he followed her in.

A moment later, Travis, Dakota, and Toby settled on the aisle side. "Where's Gavin?" Toby asked with a frown. The kid was too cute in his black vest and bow tie.

"With a sitter," she answered. She'd asked Elsie, one of her social studies students, to watch him.

"I wish I had a sitter." He gave a disgruntled look at his mama.

Dafne grinned at Dakota, who shook her head in resignation. "In a little while, bucko." She leaned past Blake to talk to Dafne. "I thought he'd like to see the pomp of the wedding, but he'd hate the reception. Apparently, he'd rather not be present at all."

"Boys." Dafne laughed.

"Hey, I resent that remark." Grinning, Blake caressed her fingers.

Dakota elbowed him lightly. "Maybe you can learn a thing or two about how this is done."

"Maybe. You never know." He didn't look at either Dakota or Dafne with his words.

It had been a month since they'd gone to Spokane for Thanksgiving, and they were heading west again in the morning. Declan had grumbled about Blake taking a few days off over Christmas, but Noah had stepped up, saying he'd cover Blake's chores.

Dafne glanced up to see Adam escort his mother to the row in front of them. Kathryn looked stunning in a silvery sequined sheath, her hair done in an updo that had taken a professional a fair bit of time, by the looks of it.

Declan trailed at his estranged wife's heels, but he nodded at Adam then entered the row first, edging past his youngest son and daughters, and taking the seat beside Alexia. Kathryn chose the aisle seat.

Made sense, probably. Nathaniel was Kathryn's son, not Declan's, for all he'd adopted her boys many years back, from what Dafne understood.

But Dafne's heart ached at the awkwardness on display

in front of her. Declan's face was set in stone, only a slight tic in his jaw revealing humanity in the tension. Alexia leaned away from her father and whispered with Ryder, while Emma tucked her hand around her mom's arm and rested her head on her shoulder. Kathryn smiled at her daughter before turning toward the front, where Noah and Adam took their places beside Nathaniel.

A hush fell over the assembly as the music swelled from the piano.

Dafne was too far down the row to get a good view until Riley appeared beside them in her gorgeous red dress, carrying white roses tucked with greenery. The bouquet covered the tiny baby bump Dafne knew existed, and the softness in Riley's eyes as she gazed at Adam caught at Dafne's heart. She shot a quick glance at Adam to see a similar expression as he watched his wife's approach.

There was a pair who'd chosen to make love an action word, for sure.

A ripple of amusement came from the back of the sanctuary as little Bella made her way to the front, flinging petals in every direction. Just as she came to the end of their aisle, she ran out of flowers and plopped down in the aisle with a huge pout on her face.

"Excuse me," whispered Dakota to Travis as she edged past him. She squatted by the toddler and whispered to her.

Bella flung her arms around Dakota's neck with a quivering sob, and Dakota cast an apologetic look toward the back of the church as she settled back into her seat, the toddler on her lap.

Really, a not-quite two-year-old was far too young to

be a flower girl, but Dafne couldn't fault Ainsley for wanting to try.

Now Vivienne strolled toward the front and took her place beside Riley. The only tell of her nervousness was a trembling bouquet as she sent a quick, lopsided grin to her twin half-sisters.

The music morphed into 'The Wedding March,' and rustles filled the space as everyone rose to honor the bride as she made her way to her groom.

Dafne would have to wait for her first glimpse of Ainsley, though she'd seen the dress a few days ago. Now, she watched the wedding party. Watched Nathaniel as he dashed tears from his eyes. She clutched Blake's hand, and he squeezed hers in return, his arm pressed tight against hers.

This was all so beautiful, so inspirational, especially knowing how difficult and heartbreaking Ainsley and Nathaniel's story had been.

Blake couldn't propose soon enough for Dafne, not now that she'd sat beside him to witness his brother's wedding. Was it too much to hope for a diamond for Christmas? It was still too soon. She knew that. But her heart wouldn't say no.

"WANT TO STEP OUTSIDE FOR A MINUTE?" Blake asked. "Full moon, and it stopped snowing — looks pretty amazing out there."

The New Year's Eve party was in full swing. They'd played cards and charades and eaten so much food Blake wasn't sure he'd need to eat for a week… although a party had never stopped him before. The countdown to midnight would be starting soon, but Blake had his own plans of how to usher in a new year.

Dafne scanned Adam and Riley's living room quickly.

"Gavin's fine. He and Toby are having a Toy Story marathon."

"Right. I'd love to." She flashed Blake a smile as she pulled on the cowboy boots he'd given her for Christmas. Gavin had been over the moon with his pair and especially the little hat.

Now, Blake grabbed Dafne's parka and helped her into it with the least fanfare possible, though a grinning Travis tossed a thumbs-up from across the room. Blake nodded at his big brother and pulled the door open.

Just being outside on a crisp night settled his spirits some. The lights from the Christmas tree glowed through the window and illuminated the covered deck. He clasped Dafne's mittened hand in his pocket as they ambled down the few steps.

"Oh, it's beautiful!" Dafne caught sight of the round moon climbing above the eastern hills.

"I thought you'd like it." There was enough light to cast a gentle glow over the snow-covered landscape. The depth of the drifts muffled the sound of the four puppies yipping in a stall in the nearby stable.

A sharp frost nipped at his nose and cheeks. They wouldn't last long out here. He turned and gathered Dafne as close as he could in her puffy parka. "I love you, beautiful." He'd positioned her so the moonlight lit her face and caught her eyes.

"I love you, too." She smiled up at him. "This was a good idea. The party's been fun, getting to know your brothers better and all that. But I'm not sad to remember the change in years with us standing out in the moonlight together."

"Seems romantic, huh?"

She looked at him quizzically. "Yeah, it does." She nestled against his chest, holding him tight.

Blake pushed her away just far enough that he could brush a kiss over her lips. His plans for New Year's memories included plenty of kissing. He cleared his throat, his heart hammering in his chest. "Dafne?"

"Hmm?"

"I can't even begin to tell you how much you mean to me."

"Right back atcha, cowboy."

"And I…" Oh, man, he was messing this up. Best just to get it out. "I want to spend the rest of my life with you at my side. Will you marry me? Please?" He fumbled in his coat pocket for the little box.

Dafne bumped his arm just as he had it half out of his pocket. She was reaching to put her arms around his neck, but the little box tumbled into the soft snow.

Time stood still.

Dafne's eyes were wide as she clapped a mittened hand to her mouth. "Blake! I'm so sorry!"

He dropped to his knees — probably this was a sign he should have been down there, anyway — and felt around for the velvet box. Where was it?

A second later, the area was illuminated by Dafne's flashlight app, and he saw the black box. Good thing he hadn't gone for a white one, or it might not have surfaced again until spring. Or, at least, daylight.

With a sigh of relief, he tipped the lid back and showed her the diamond glistening in the flashlight glow.

"Blake, that's beautiful. I'm so sorry I knocked it from your hand." The artificial light went out as she pocketed her phone.

"No harm done, sweetheart. My tailbone is fine this time. My pride is fine... unless your answer is no. Then..." Blake swallowed hard at the thought of what her rejection would do to him. No. She wouldn't turn him down. Would she?

"Yes. I say yes." She cradled his face between her fluffy mittens, bent down, and kissed him gently.

He tugged her left mitten off and carefully plucked the ring from its nest. It would never do to drop *that* in the snow. But he got it safely in its place and kissed her knuckles.

Dafne helped him to his feet. "Blake, I love you so much. Gavin and I are blessed and honored to have you in our life."

"I'm the one who's honored, sweetheart. I wasn't looking for a ready-made family, but that's exactly what God blessed me with. I can't wait to begin our life together."

"Soon," she whispered against his lips. "Now kiss me like you mean it, cowboy."

"Oh, Dafne..." And he proceeded to show her exactly how much she meant to him.

EPILOGUE

Noah let himself out of his brother's house and into the cold night air. It was New Year's Eve, and the brothers had gathered for a party. At least, some of them. After the wedding, Nathaniel and Ainsley had gone for an overnight to Missoula before returning to spend Christmas with Bella. Now they were off for a week in Belize while Vivienne and Bella stayed with Mom and the twins. One big happy houseful, or something.

Nathaniel's wedding had been... nice. Both Noah's brothers were married now. So was Travis and, minutes ago, Blake and Dafne had returned to the house after a moonlight stroll during which Blake had popped the question and a glowing Dafne had said yes.

Soon it would be just Noah and Ryder left. Ryder might be a full five years younger than Noah, but with his kind of luck, the younger guy would likely get married first.

Noah trudged across the yard to the stable where he could hear the puppies scuffling in the bed of hay he'd freshened for them earlier. By his best guess, they were about three months old now. Billy was Adam and Riley's dog, and Blake had taken Salem.

That left two for Noah, since he hadn't been able to find homes for them. He hadn't tried that hard, truth be told. The guys teased him about having a soft spot for anyone in distress, puppies included, and it was hard to deny. His dad's death when he was only eleven had hit him hard, and it was only by God's grace he'd gotten through that period in his life, made incredibly more difficult by Mom's marriage to Declan a year later.

The puppies swarmed his ankles as he let himself into their box stall. He settled into the hay himself, his back against the wall, as they tumbled all over his lap and growled at his boots. Seconds later, Deidre curled up in his lap and fell asleep like someone had flipped her light switch off.

He ran his fingers over her silky ears as the other three settled tight against him, each forming a warm, round ball. Then he leaned back and looked up to the ceiling.

"Lord? You out there?"

Of course, he knew God was present. A God who loved him, who'd called him, who wanted the best for him. But a restlessness was growing. Noah was twenty-eight, and he'd never had a real girlfriend. Never been in love. He wasn't as shy as his twin, and even Nat had managed to find and marry the woman of his dreams.

But not Noah. Every time he'd begun to gather courage to ask a woman out, it turned out she was already half in love with someone else. Like Tori Carmichael over in Saddle Springs. She'd been married to Garrett Morrison for a couple of years now. She was happy — Noah still shod their horses as part of his circuit, still saw them regularly.

Was there anyone out there for him? If not, it might be nice to know. He'd keep the farrier business instead of selling it, keep being a nomad with no real home. But if God had someone for him, he'd appreciate knowing that, too. It'd give Noah a nudge out of his shell so he'd snap up his bride before some other guy got there first.

"God? How about You make it really clear?"

"Make what really clear?" Ryder's voice came from above the stall's half-door.

Heat shot up Noah's face. How had he not heard Ryder coming in? He shrugged. "Nothing."

"Yeah, I bet. I'd ask what you're doing out here, but I suspect I know. There's an awful lot of mush going on inside the house right now. A guy needs a break from it all."

"You're not completely wrong." The difference was that Noah wished he were part of it, while Ryder didn't seem to. "But I wanted to check on the pups."

"Sure, you did." Ryder laughed. "They're fine. See?"

"I'm gonna take my two and head back to Rockstead in a few minutes. Call it a night."

"Yeah. Happy New Year, bro. May all your dreams come true."

And Ryder didn't even sound sarcastic, for once.

"You, too."

A NOTE

Dear Noah,

You've been a favorite of mine since you strolled into the Saddle Springs Romance series in *The Cowboy's Belated Discovery*, busily shoeing horses at the Carmichael family's guest ranch. I didn't know your brothers much at that point, though Adam became an integral part of *The Cowboy's Reluctant Bride*.

I saw your heart for your younger sisters. I saw your caution around women, even through your friendship with Tori Carmichael. I saw your worry over your mom's depression. I know you're proud of her transition in recent months as she's begun to take control of her life. And I know you're praying for your stepdad and a resolution for their marriage.

I've been curious what made you tick for a couple of years now, and I can't wait to get to know you more deeply. You may think you're too much a loner and have too much wanderlust to settle down like your brothers, but let's see what we can do about that.

Reach for the future in *Choose Me for Always, Cowboy!*
~Your Loving Author, Valerie

Dear Reader,

Did you miss the previous Cavanagh brothers' stories? You'll find all them all at valeriecomer.com/cavanagh.

ACKNOWLEDGMENTS

Ah, cowboys! There's just something about them, isn't there? Masculine, hardworking, resourceful, honorable, and gentlemanly... a cowboy is hard to beat.

Thank YOU, dear reader, for loving the Saddle Springs Romance series so much I was inspired to write the Cavanagh Cowboys Romance series as a spin-off. I hope you enjoy the ride. Pun intended!

Always, always, thanks to my fellow author and friend, Elizabeth Maddrey. She prods, cheers, and commiserates as needed, then offers helpful brainstorming and critiques. If you haven't read her Christian contemporary romances, go find them and get started!

My amazing editor, Nicole, has been with me from the beginning. She went above and beyond the call of duty this time, going through the manuscript not once, not twice, but three times before she felt I'd 'nailed it.' I am so thankful for her!

I'm also grateful for the Christian Indie Authors Facebook group and my sister bloggers at Inspy Romance.

These folks make a difference in my life every single day. I'm thrilled to walk beside them as we tell stories for Jesus!

Thank you to my Facebook friends, followers, street team, and reader group members for prayers, encouragement, and great fellowship. If you'd like to join other readers who love my stories, please find us at Valerie Comer: Readers Group.

Thanks to my husband, Jim, whose love for me never fails and who encourages me in every endeavor. Thanks to my kids, their spouses, and my wonderful grandgirls for cheering me on. To them, having an author for a mom/grandma is "normal." Imagine that!

All my love and gratitude goes to Jesus, the One who is my vision, the High King of Heaven, the lord of my heart. Thank You. A thousand times, thank You.

ABOUT VALERIE COMER

Valerie Comer's life on a small farm in western Canada provides the seed for stories of contemporary Christian romance. Like many of her characters, Valerie grows much of her own food and is active in the local foods movement as well as her church. She only hopes her imaginary friends enjoy their happily-ever-afters as much as she does hers, shared with her husband, adult kids, and adorable grandkids.

Valerie is a *USA Today* bestselling author and a two-time Word Award winner. She writes engaging characters, strong communities, and deep faith into her green clean romances.

To find out more, visit her website at www.valeriecomer.com, where you can read her blog, explore her many links, and sign up for her email newsletter, where you will find news, giveaways, deals, book recommendations and more. You can also find Valerie blogging with other authors of Christian contemporary romance at Inspy Romance.